SYSTEMA PARADOXA

ACCOUNTS OF CRYPTOZOOLOGICAL IMPORT

VOLUME 23
SKEPTIC SOUP
A TALE OF THE GUGWE

AS ACCOUNTED BY MICHAEL A. VENTRELLA

NEOPARADOXA
Pennsville, NJ
2024

PUBLISHED BY
NeoParadoxa
A division of eSpec Books
PO Box 242
Pennsville, NJ 08070
www.especbooks.com

ISBN: 978-1-956463-75-0
ISBN (ebook): 978-1-956463-74-3

Interior Design: Danielle McPhail
www.sidhenadaire.com

Cover Art: JW Harp
Cover Design: Mike and Danielle McPhail, McP Digital Graphics
Interior Illustration: JW Harp

Copyediting: Greg Schauer and John L. French

DEDICATION

Dedicated to my family:
Wife, Heidi Hooper,
and cats, Mrs. Premise, Mrs. Conclusion,
Doctor Who, and River Song.

CHAPTER ONE

"Are you sure it's steady?"

Malcolm was glad that from behind the camera, Barry couldn't see his eyes rolling. He glanced over at Prisha, who shared a knowing moment with him, then turned to Barry and gave him a thumbs up.

"Yes, of course it is," she said to Barry. "I know what I'm doing, okay? It's already recording, so start whenever you want."

Barry turned on his video smile and jumped up and down a bit to get pumped, all in preparation for the show. "Build up the tension!" he said, like he always did before recording, reminding himself and his partners to keep everything exciting for the viewers and listeners.

"Three... two... one..."

He held open his hands. "And with that theme music out of the way, welcome again to another edition of 'Skeptic Soup,' the show where we debunk the supernatural and superstitious. I am Barry Lowery, your host. As you know from our last show, we proved that the Ghost of Pine Hollow was a mere optical illusion caused by the sun hitting an indoor mirror at the correct angle. Many who live in Pine Hollow are not convinced, but that's normal among those who do not have the ability to see the facts laid before them."

Malcolm had to admit that of the three of them, Barry was the most telegenic and perfect for the job as host. Blond hair, bright eyes, and a smile that otherwise could have made him a game show emcee or the anchor of the nightly news. He was also the most stubborn man he had ever met, ready to argue with anyone he thought held the wrong opinion—that is, any opinion that was different than his. He tended to be too insulting to those who believed, instead of understanding them. But hey, Barry paid the bills, and they did get to travel a lot.

He watched as Prisha checked the digital camera on the cheap tripod before her. The makeup highlighting her eyes made her look like a panda to Malcolm—but a cute, cuddly one you wanted to hug. Her dark hair was cut short at the shoulders, matching her black lipstick, but what really made her stand out was her love of black clothing and the skull earrings dangling over her shoulders. Goth Skeptic Soup fans tuned in most of the time just to watch her. No complaints there—all the better for the numbers.

Barry continued on. "And today, we're up in Canada to investigate a creature known as 'the Gugwe.' Before I tell you what our plan is, allow me to once again introduce our expert investigator, Malcolm Pulley. Malcolm, come on over here!"

Malcolm pasted on a smile and walked into camera range. "Hi, everyone." He waved. "It's a lot colder up here in Canada."

Barry nudged him. "What have you discovered about this thing, Malcolm?"

Malcolm adjusted his glasses. "Well, the Gugwe is one of what is known as a cryptid—a mysterious creature that is seldom seen, like Bigfoot. Reports have it as a bipedal creature with a wolf-like snout. Sightings of the creature go back at least a hundred years or so, maybe more. Unlike Bigfoot, it's said to be aggressive and will attack people."

"We'll get to that in a minute," Barry added.

"Yes. Well." Malcolm scratched his nose. "It's been photographed a few times, although the pictures are blurry and not very insightful. It seems to have a sagittal crest, which gives it an elongated head, like a gorilla. And, of course, there are no gorillas in this area."

"Pictures can be misleading when seen at a bad angle," Barry said. "They were most likely a bear, right? Or some kid dressed up trying to fool us?"

"Anything's possible," Malcolm replied. "Then again, gorillas were considered cryptids until one was actually captured, so…"

"That was a more primitive time!" Barry said.

Malcolm leaned toward the camera to prevent Barry from taking over his section of the show. "But here's the interesting part to me. Ten thousand years ago or so, there was a 'short-nosed bear' scientists called '*Arctodus simus*.' It was huge, like ten feet tall, and massive. Based on bones and fossils discovered, it lived in this area." He looked straight at the camera. "What if it *didn't* go extinct? What if—"

"Tell us about the Woodbooger," Barry interrupted. "I love that name!"

Malcolm glared at Barry for a second, realized he was still being recorded, and turned on his professional face. "The so-called 'Woodbooger' is similar to the Gugwe and may even be the same creature. Reports of that one say the face is more chimpanzee-like, but the two could be related."

"Except they don't exist," Barry prompted.

"As far as we know."

"And that's what this episode will be about," Barry said to the camera. "Proving they don't exist!"

"The Woodbooger's been seen in northern Virginia," Malcolm said. "Quite a long distance from Quebec. More likely the Gugwe is related to the Sasquatch, which has a more human-like face, and is common in Canada."

"But let's talk about why we're here now," Barry said, clearly trying to steer the conversation away. "The alleged attack! And here to report on that is Prisha Singh."

Prisha stepped before the camera. Malcolm noted Barry's stare against the back of her head. He never said anything, but it was clear Barry didn't like the fact that Prisha received more fan emails and comments than he did.

Prisha refrained from smiling, given the news she had to report. "A week or so ago, a group of teenagers claimed they saw the Gugwe in an area called 'Les Sept-Chutes' or 'the seven waterfalls' in English. It made a scary noise at them and they dashed away, but once they felt safe, they looked back and, you know, realized one of their friends was missing. Police were called and a search took place, but nothing was found. The search has continued, although not as prominent as before, and we hope to be able to speak to those kids and the police as a part of our investigation."

Malcolm decided he needed to speak. "I don't think the kids are pulling a hoax. They wouldn't have their friend hide for this long just to pull a trick."

"If the friend even existed in the first place!" Barry said.

"Well, I assume the police have already checked that out..." Malcolm said.

"Of course, and the grieving family can't be a part of this as well," Prisha added. "The kid actually existed. Or still exists, we don't know yet."

Barry waved them away and turned to the camera. "And that's what we will investigate next, so be sure to check out our upcoming episode when we'll have more news for you. 'Skeptic Soup' is brought to you by grants from American Atheists and The Association for Skeptical Inquiry, so be sure to support them with your donations so we can continue. If you want to support us directly, go to our Patreon page where you can see outtakes and download our written research. Click the code on your screen now. You can also buy Skeptic Soup t-shirts and coffee cups to show your support! And don't forget to 'like,' and 'subscribe' for future updates. Have something to say? Post your comments below and share this with your friends. With Malcolm Pulley and Prisha Singh, I'm Barry Lowery with Skeptic Soup!"

He continued smiling for at least five seconds and pointed a finger at his companions. "You shouldn't be contradicting me like that," he said. "We're supposed to be attacking these things."

"But there really is a missing kid," Malcolm said. "I'm worried for him."

"It was probably a bear, you know, and in the excitement, they all imagined something else," Prisha said as she packed up the camera. "Being a skeptic doesn't mean you refuse to believe actual facts, like a missing kid."

"Our job is to make an exciting show that gathers views, donations, and ads," Barry said. "Especially now that the Discovery Channel has expressed an interest in us. We need to have a coherent view. Malcolm practically said that this stupid thing could actually exist."

Prisha removed the camera from the tripod. She'd edit everything together later with the theme music and logo before posting it. "Our job is to be skeptics, and that means being skeptical even about things we want strongly to believe. Do I think this thing exists? No, of course not. But, you know, I'm also skeptical about that belief. If we find proof the thing does exist, then the evidence will change my mind. That's what being a skeptic means, you know. Otherwise, you're just a contrarian."

Malcolm watched Barry fume silently for a few seconds, and then Barry took a deep breath and spoke. "Fine, just edit this thing and post it. We'll get back to the motel and sleep it off, and then try to see if those kids will talk to us tomorrow."

"A good plan," Malcolm said. "I'm exhausted from the drive, pretty as it was."

Chapter Two

After spending the night on an uncomfortable motel mattress, trying to sleep through both a raging thunderstorm and Barry's snoring in the adjoining bed, Malcolm needed coffee. He sipped at the small opening on the plastic cover and then zipped up his jacket a bit more against the brisk morning.

"This is really good," he said, munching on a Tim Horton's doughnut. "You guys don't want to try? It's maple frosted or something."

"Don't tempt me," Prisha said. "It's not like I want to be gluten-free."

"Maybe later," Barry replied, eyes on the road.

Malcolm took another bite. "More for me. And we need to get some more to take back to Boston. I mean, I love Dunkin' as much as any other person, but maybe if I show my friends this…"

Barry snorted but didn't respond.

Malcolm finished his donut and concentrated on the day's plan. He had tried to contact the teenagers that he saw on the news program, but only one was willing to speak to the crew—a nerdy-looking dweeb with blue-framed glasses and hair that jutted out from his head like it was trying to escape. Malcolm was looking forward to meeting the kid. He looked interesting.

Barry and Prisha, however, were still angry at each other after their argument the night before. Cautiously, Malcolm approached the subject. "Was a decision made?"

"Yes!" Prisha said at the same time Barry yelled, "No!"

Malcolm closed his eyes for a second and then took another sip of coffee.

"Turn left in half a kilometer," the GPS lady said over the van's speakers, muting the '70s progressive rock Barry always played.

Malcolm couldn't tell one of those bands from another. Rush? Styx? Yes? Some other one-word band name? Who knew? Malcolm was never into the oldies.

"Look, this kid is much more likely to tell me what's going on than he'll tell you," Prisha said to Barry, resuming the argument. "You have this look on your face when you don't believe people, you know."

"Me? A look?"

"Yes! That look right there!" She pointed at him. "That's the look that says, 'I can't believe what you're telling me!' Haven't you realized by now after all the shows we've done that that doesn't work? All it does, you know, is make your interviewee put up their defenses and often refuse to answer you."

Barry laughed. "Of course, because they've been called out on their bullshit! They realize they can't pull one over on me. It makes for a great visual, doesn't it?"

Her mouth tightened. "Maybe, when we know we're dealing with a charlatan who's trying to profit off some supernatural scam. But this time, it's a kid who's missing his friend and is very scared. I think he's mistaken as to what he saw, but, you know, I don't think he's trying to pull a scam. I mean, what does he have to gain from this? Why would he lie about it?"

Barry shook his head from side to side for a few moments before replying. "I can be calmer. I can do this."

Prisha glanced back at Malcolm, who shrugged without commitment. Not his fight.

"He's also a young kid with hormones. A pretty girl could maybe get more out of him," she offered.

Barry laughed. "With our luck, he's probably gay."

"What if he only speaks French?" Prisha added. "I did take French in college, you know. Did you?"

Barry snorted but didn't answer as Prisha looked back at Malcolm again, eyes wide, begging him to speak up.

Malcolm took a deep breath. "I agree with Prisha. I think we can get better answers from the kid if she's asking the questions. Especially if he mostly speaks French. Even if he is gay."

"Oh, so is this the 'Prisha Singh' show now?" Barry loudly said. "A pretty girl is more important than a good reporter? Besides, Prisha says 'you know' too much. It's distracting."

"I do not!" She pouted, and then quietly asked, "do I?"

"It's not that distracting," Malcolm said. "We should do what will give us information best. She should talk."

Barry turned faster than he should, making Malcolm grab his coffee tighter to prevent it from spilling through that little hole. "Fine!" Barry said. "Let's do that, then. I'll just sit in the van since I have nothing to do."

"Good idea," Prisha said.

"Build up the tension," Barry said, half under his breath.

No one spoke for the rest of the ride.

Malcolm spent the time staring out the window, determined to enjoy the beautiful autumn scenery. They had left their nice little motel, about six or seven miles from Les Sept-Chutes Park, and were now passing by farmlands whose crops had long since been harvested. Malcolm was interested in seeing the park's beauty. The only way to do so, according to the pamphlet he picked up at a Subway shop, is by hiking up the hills to see the falls themselves. Hopefully, that would be part of the investigation.

In any event, the person they were planning to interview lived about twenty kilometers away, in a small town called "Sainte-Émélie-de-l'Énergie." Prisha said that translated roughly as "Saint Emile of Energy," much to Malcolm's amusement. He kept imagining some weird steampunk town with mad scientists running around yelling "Eureka!"

Malcolm spent the next few minutes trying to remember how to convert kilometers into miles, but eventually gave up.

He kept his nose to the window, determined to not let the tension in the van distract him from appreciating the view. The vastness of the scenery was quite a change from the cityscape he was used to, or even the caves he liked to explore in his spare time.

Malcolm had arranged the interview with the young man and knew he could speak English just fine, but with an obvious French accent which made Malcolm think any minute he would say, "Your mother was a hamster and your father smelt of elderberries." Nathan Leblanc was the kid's name. His mother had been very protective of him and had only agreed to the interview when she was assured that they were doing a documentary on the disappearance and would be respectful to Nathan and his friends. After all, both Nathan and his mother wanted nothing more than to find the missing boy.

Knowing Barry would never be able to comfort these people in their stressful time, Malcolm was glad that Barry had given in. He hoped Barry would keep his word and stay out of it.

CHAPTER THREE

Nathan was just a kid. He looked around fifteen years old, with acne and braces and glasses that were too small for his round face. His eyes were big and darted from Malcolm to Prisha and back again, while his mother talked nonstop in broken English. Malcolm nodded his head in response, catching most of the words but all of the meaning.

Prisha kept busy setting up the cameras and doing mic checks. There would be one camera situated behind Prisha's head, showing Nathan, and another showing the two of them together. Malcolm's job was to monitor the cameras while holding his phone and recording the best he could from the side, just in case one of the other cameras didn't have the best view or best sound. Prisha would use her computer magic to edit it all together later.

She had switched into what she called her "boring get-up" — no dark make-up, no dangling skulls... just a professional tan skirt, thin white blouse with the top buttons undone, and matching tan jacket that made her appear to be the kind of journalist that populates cable TV. She knew that she needed this look for certain interviews to go smoothly, and as much as she hated the disguise, she wore it without noticeable discomfort. Malcolm admired her acting skills, as he knew she hated that look.

They were outside to take advantage of the morning light. Prisha spent a few minutes rearranging the chairs to eliminate any shadows covering Nathan's face or sunlight causing reflections in his glasses, and then announced that she was satisfied.

Nathan's mother continued on. "...And the only reason I am letting you do this is because you have promised that you are filming for a, what is it called, documentary? Documentary is to help find Phillipe, the poor boy. My boy was so scared and worried, and you want to help, no? Just do not upset him or interview is over, yes? You understand?"

Malcolm nodded again as Prisha sat in her interviewing chair. She reached into a pocket and pulled out her phone, opened the photo app, and examined her make-up and hair, using the app as a mirror.

The breeze was pleasant enough, but a bit chilly on this autumn day. However, they were in a beautiful countryside, with tall evergreen trees hiding the more colorful ones changing their leaves for the tourists, and it was hard to be depressed over a chill.

The pleasant little town was set up to take advantage of tourists and campers, and Prisha and Malcolm were surprised to find shops selling Gugwe gifts, mostly of a humorous bent. It reminded him of the time Skeptic Soup did a story about Rachel, Nevada, the "UFO capital of the world." Situated near the U.S. Government's "Area 51," tourists and UFO nuts proved to be just the thing that place needed to prevent it from becoming a ghost town.

Despite all the vast and empty surrounding land and forests, good old Saint Emile of Energy tried to squeeze as many homes as possible into the smallest area. Nearby neighbors watched from porches and windows. Nathan's backyard worked fine for the interview, since it was fenced in, preventing any neighborhood dogs or curious onlookers from disturbing them.

Prisha's tight top was distracting, Malcolm had to admit, and it appeared to work, as Nathan kept his eyes on her the entire time. Hopefully, her theory that this would help keep Nathan talking would prove to be true.

"Are you ready, Nathan?" she asked as she held the mic toward him.

"Yes, Miss Prisha," he said, as he ran his fingers through his long hair.

She motioned for him to take the lawn chair his mother had placed out for him. Keeping him comfortable and relaxed was the best way to get information out of him.

"Okay, Nathan. I'm going to ask you some questions. Be sure to look at me as you answer, even if Malcolm here is moving the other camera around. This is not an interrogation, you know, so if you want to take a break at any time, just say the word. I want you to be comfortable. I know some people in the media have made fun of the idea that you were attacked by a Gugwe, but we're here to investigate that, and no one is going to laugh at you now. Okay?"

Nathan nodded. "Okay."

"Then we'll start." She gave a little cough to clear her throat, and then motioned for Malcolm to turn on the cameras. Malcolm went to the two on the tripods and switched them on, then clicked on his phone and nodded to Prisha. Prisha remained still for a few seconds and then began.

"I'm here with Nathan Leblanc, who was—*is* friends with Phillipe. Nathan was there when Phillipe disappeared. Hello, Nathan."

"Hello."

"Tell us about yourself, Nathan. You're a student?"

"Yes."

"What's your favorite subject?"

Nathan's eyebrows shot up. "Oh. Um. Science, I guess. Maybe music."

"Oh!" Prisha smiled. "What instrument do you play?"

"Saxophone."

"That's a great instrument! And lots of bands love to have saxophone players."

"Yeah, I'm in the marching band."

"Who's your favorite saxophone player?"

Malcolm knew that Prisha asked these preliminary questions to make Nathan feel more comfortable before getting into the details. Since most of this would be edited out for the show, his mind wandered and before he realized, a few minutes had passed, and Prisha was finally getting to the important stuff.

"So tell me about your friends. You went out with them a week or so ago, right? Who else was there besides you and Phillippe?"

Nathan looked very sad, and Malcolm felt his chest tighten. This poor kid. He wasn't faking this or lying for attention. He probably just saw a bear, but that doesn't mean he wasn't scared.

Nathan's mother stood behind Malcolm, watching closely and remaining silent.

"John and Eric," Nathan said. "The four of us go to the falls a lot, just to hang out and stuff. There wasn't nothing unusual about it."

"Was the weather nice?"

"Oh, yeah. Beautiful day. That's why we went out. Rode our bikes up there, and then we sat and made fun of the tourists."

Prisha laughed. "In front of them?"

Nathan looked shocked. "Oh, no. We just sit on a rock and make jokes about them from a distance."

Prisha nodded understandingly. "So, what happened on this day? Why didn't any tourists see what you saw?"

"'Cause they weren't there." Nathan clasped his hands before him and looked over Prisha's shoulder, avoiding eye contact. He took some time before answering, as if he wasn't sure he should be talking. "Well, *we* weren't there. We didn't do it that day. We didn't go to the falls. We—we got this place we set up near one of the falls. It's like a little camp, far away from any tourists. We brought some wood and made a little tree house and stuff. No one even knew it was there." He looked down at his feet. "I shouldn't have said that," he mumbled.

"That sounds, you know, fantastic!" Prisha gushed. Malcolm wondered if she was being a bit too enthusiastic and that Nathan would suspect she didn't really mean it, but Nathan kept talking.

"Yeah, it's a good place to cool down and relax," he said, looking up at Prisha. "We never lit a fire or anything though, 'cause we knew the rangers would see the smoke."

"Smart," Prisha said. "So where exactly is it?"

Nathan's eyes widened. "I can't tell you. I shouldn't have even said what I did. We all made a promise never to tell anyone where it was."

"Did you tell the police?"

Nathan shook his head. "No, we just said we were wandering in the woods and got lost so we couldn't say exactly where it happened. We didn't want them to find it and get mad at us or anything."

"You didn't tell the police?" Nathan's mother stormed into the picture. "You didn't even tell *me*! Don't you think that's an important piece of information?"

"Mom! I made a promise!"

"A boy is missing, and if the police knew about this site, it might have helped them find him!" She shook her head. "As soon as this interview is done, we are going to call the police.."

Nathan looked aghast. "But we'll be in trouble..."

His mother frowned. "You're already in trouble with me, no?" She spoke quickly in French and Malcolm imagined it was not pleasant for Nathan, who squirmed uncomfortably. She then turned to Prisha and apologized for interrupting the recording.

Nathan stared at the ground and grunted his displeasure.

Prisha smiled. "Don't worry, Nathan, we can edit all that out. And we can tell the police about it for you. They don't have to know where we got the information, okay? We promise to do it as soon as we're done here. After all, this is very important and we all want to find Phillippe. Is that okay, Mrs. LeBlanc?"

She nodded her agreement. "They need to be told."

Prisha smiled, waited a few seconds to allow for a better edit, and then said to Nathan, "So let's talk about this place, since the secret is out. Where is it?"

Nathan took some time before answering, and when he did, his voice was so low that Malcolm had to strain to listen. "You have to go to this dirt road about half a kilometer before the main entrance, and after a ways, you'll see these huge rocks that look like big…" He paused and turned red. "Well, um, they look like two big boobs, next to each other. That kind of got our attention, 'cause it's so funny. We call it 'Boobie Rock.'"

Prisha laughed. "That would be a good name for your band."

Nathan grinned in response, his nervousness fading. "Anyway, you can't see our spot from the road, but there's another smaller path behind the rocks that goes up the side of the hill toward the falls. It's not really a path, more of a ditch where water runs after a big rain or when snow melts. Anyway, we have to walk the bikes at that point, especially since it's uphill. You can hear and feel the falls as you get there, but it's so far from everything that no one can see it."

"So you guys were there hanging out?" Prisha asked. "Smoking some weed?"

Nathan turned red again and looked toward his mother. Malcolm didn't turn around to see her expression.

"Well, yeah, sometimes Phillippe brings it, 'cause he's older. But it's not like you think. It's legal here, you know."

"But you're supposed to be nineteen first," his mother said. "No wonder you didn't tell me. I wonder what else you're hiding."

Nathan blushed.

Prisha smiled. "We can edit that part out, Nathan, don't worry. So let's talk about what you saw. Can you describe it for me?"

Nathan looked at his feet. "I've told so many people already…"

"Yes, but we're here to try to find Phillippe and solve this mystery. So maybe there's something new you haven't already said that could make a difference. And maybe we're more likely to believe you and help you find the Gugwe."

"I don't think that's a good idea. I mean ... I mean, look at Phillippe."

Prisha leaned forward and gently placed a hand on Nathan's knee. "We need to prove to everyone that you aren't making something up or, you know, were high and thinking a bear was a Gugwe."

He didn't look up but nodded his agreement. "It wasn't a bear."

Prisha gave Malcolm a glance and then turned back to Nathan. "How can you be sure?"

Nathan gave her a frustrated look. "I live here. I see bears all the time. I know what a bear looks like. This wasn't a bear."

"Fair enough," Prisha said. "So tell us what happened."

Nathan shifted in his seat. "We were just sitting around, goofing off, talking sh… stuff, doing nothing… just hanging out. Eric said we should head back soon because it was starting to get dark, and especially there in the woods where the sun don't shine much. And we never light fires there because then the rangers would see the smoke. So we were gathering up our things when we heard something in the woods." He paused, his eyes unfocused.

"What did it sound like?" Prisha prodded.

"Like a low grumble, but also someone big walking through the sticks and stuff." Nathan spread his hands. "We just thought maybe it was the police or the park rangers and we'd be in trouble for making our camp and smoking. We didn't say nothing, but we were smart enough to try not to make noise or something. So we went to our bikes but had just gotten there when…"

Prisha waited for him to continue, but after a few more long seconds of silence, said, "It's okay, Nathan. You can do this."

Nathan nodded to himself but kept his view to the ground. "It just burst through the trees, and there it was. It made this screeching kind of sound. I can't really describe it, 'cause it was both, like, screechy and deep at the same time."

"What did it look like? Can you describe it?"

"Really tall. Hairy. No clothes. Stood upright, not like a bear stands upright, but like a person stands upright. But the face was like a dog, but a warped, weird dog. Not a real dog. Kind of crushed, like those dogs that have those little noses that look like they ran into a door. You know the ones I mean? Like that, but big and scary." He took a deep breath.

"Anyway, it's not like I stayed to look at it. I dropped the bike and just ran down the hill."

Prisha patted Nathan's hand. "What about the other boys?"

Nathan reached up and wiped at his eyes. Prisha was ready, and handed him a tissue, which he used, and then blew his nose. "Sorry," he said in a cracked voice. "I've told this to the police and the rangers and everyone so many times, and it's still hard. I feel terrible." He looked straight at Prisha. "I don't know what happened to the other boys. I was so scared, I just ran. I couldn't even think. When I got to the main trail, I looked back, and Eric and John were running to meet me, but we didn't see Phillippe."

"What did you do?"

"We called his name a bunch of times, and then ran to the ranger station." He gave a slight shrug. "Well, we kind of ran. It's like we had this extra power but after a while, it ran out and we just jogged, we were so, I don't know, stressed or something. It's not like the ranger station was close."

"You told the rangers everything?"

"Yeah. They didn't believe us at first, but it didn't take long for them to realize we were really scared and weren't faking it." He held his hand out for another tissue, which Prisha provided. After wiping his eyes and nose, he added, "I never went back. I was too scared. My bike's still there. That's kind of all I know."

"Did the police find anything?"

Nathan gave a shrug. "Nothing more than what you've seen on the news. They've searched the woods. I don't know if they found our hiding place. No Phillipe."

Prisha looked like she was about to ask something, then paused and tilted her head down while keeping her eyes on Nathan. "Tell me about Phillipe. What was he like?"

Nathan held his hands together. "He's the oldest one. In grade twelve."

"So a senior?"

"What? No, he's just turned eighteen. He's not a senior citizen."

"We don't use those terms here, Prisha," said Nathan's mother. "It's just 'grade twelve.'"

"Ah, sorry." Prisha gave a big smile. "Please continue, Nathan. You were telling me about Phillippe."

"Yeah, okay. Um. So he just turned eighteen. He plays drums, and we have a sort of band, although we never played anywhere yet. He likes anime and Avatar—the cartoon, not the blue people thing. He loves to play practical jokes. One time, he had me convinced that my turtle was growing and then shrinking, but then I found out he'd been switching my turtle with other ones when I wasn't looking. His parents are divorced but his mom works in a pet store. That's where he got the turtles. He has a sister who plays hockey. Um. I'm not sure what else I can say."

"No, that's good." Prisha smiled. "You need to keep his memory strong."

"You say that like he's dead!"

"No, I say that like he's gone. When he comes back, he'll be glad to know you thought of him."

Nathan wiped at his eyes again. "Is that enough? Are we done?"

Prisha looked back at Malcolm, who nodded his agreement.

"Yes, Nathan. Thank you so much for this information. We really appreciate it."

Malcolm turned off the phone and began packing up the equipment as Prisha made small talk with Nathan's mother. So, Phillippe was a practical joker, was he?

CHAPTER FOUR

Barry didn't help load anything back into the van, but just sat in the driver's seat, flipping through his iPad. It was only once everything was packed away and Malcolm and Prisha took their seats that he acknowledged them by placing his arm on the seat and turning to face them both.

"So how did it go? Did he confess?"

"Don't be ridiculous," Prisha said. "You think after being interviewed by Mounties or whatever they call them here that he would suddenly admit a hoax to some stranger?"

Barry grinned. "Hey, you're the one who said a pretty girl would get him to confess."

Prisha crossed her arms. "I said no such thing."

"The important thing," Malcolm said, hoping to defuse the conversation, "is that we learned a bit more about the other kids, including the fact that Phillippe, the missing one, is a big practical joker." He twisted the top off his iced coffee and took a sip.

"Aha!" Barry said, eyebrows raised. "This goes along with what I've been researching while you two were out there interviewing." He pointed to the screen. "Apparently, this Gugwe thing is good for business. There have been other sightings over the years, and each time, attendance at the park grows."

"Yeah, we know," Malcolm said. "We saw the tourist stuff in town earlier while you were driving."

Barry sniffed. "Should have said something."

Prisha held up a hand. "Wait. Let me get this straight. Are you implying that a government-run national park would fake a missing child to get more tourists here? A non-profit park? Where the people running it don't get any of the income from park fees?"

"No," Barry said, slowly and deliberately, as if speaking to a child. "But who would profit from this? All the local businesses in this small town. Tourists need places to stay and food and souvenirs and crap, right?"

He readjusted his seat position, strapped on his seat belt, and started up the van. "We have a motive." He looked in his mirrors and then pulled out onto the road.

"You're ignoring the fact that an eighteen-year-old kid has been missing for more than a week now," Malcolm said. "He's still in school, and he has a family. You think they're all a part of this? That they're hiding him? It's not like he has the money to go hide by himself."

"Besides, his mother runs a pet store," Prisha said. "She wouldn't benefit from tourism."

"You never know, because… hey! Move your ass!" Barry shook his head. "Damn, these Canadian drivers are just as bad as the ones in Boston. I swear, they're so polite until you get them on the road…"

"Or on a hockey court," Malcolm added with a grin.

"Is it called a court?" Prisha bit her lip. "Or maybe an arena?"

"Maybe it's a rink," Malcolm said. "Like a skating rink."

"It doesn't matter," Barry said, "My point was… what was my point? Oh, right. If the businesses in the town all agreed to do this at some town meeting or something, then maybe Phillippe's mom would have gone along with it."

"Will you listen to yourself?" Prisha said. "We're Skeptic Soup. We're always talking about how almost all conspiracy theories are nonsense, because people just can't keep big secrets like that for long."

Malcolm held up his coffee as if it was a prop proving a point. "Yeah, and how the more people in a conspiracy, the more likely it will be exposed."

"You can't deny that conspiracies do exist sometimes, though," Barry said. "Especially with businesses. They conspire all the time to set prices and influence legislation…"

"Well, let's keep that as a background theory but not talk about it on the show unless we have proof," Prisha said. "That's what being a skeptic means, after all. If we talked about conspiracies like that, half of our viewers would flood the comments sections with bad reviews."

Barry waived his hand dismissively. "For now, I agree. But don't discount the possibility. I mean, even if the 'conspiracy' is just one businessperson and Phillippe."

"You're reaching for something that probably doesn't exist," Prisha said. "And where are we going, anyway? This isn't the way back to the motel."

Barry smiled. "While you were interviewing the kid, I made an appointment with one of the park rangers who agreed to be on camera. She seemed very nice, but wanted to make it clear that the purpose of our interview would only be to get the word out in case anyone has any information that could help find Phillippe. Her name is Sophie... something. I can't remember her last name."

"That'll be good for the show," Prisha admitted. "I assume you want to interview her yourself. You don't think she's part of the conspiracy, do you?"

"Don't worry, I won't screw this up." Barry hit the turn signal. "I want to ask her about where the sighting was and so on."

"Oh, we have some information about that," Malcolm said. "Let's see if what we learn from the ranger matches what the kid said."

"Why?" Barry asked as he turned into the park's lot, which was crowded with cars. He drove slowly, looking for a spot. "What did he say that we don't already know?"

Prisha pointed toward an empty spot. "The kids set up a little camp with a tree fort thing that the adults didn't know about. He told us basically how to find it, too."

"Well, that's something!" Barry seemed happy and anxious. "We'll have to check that out after we... wait a minute, what's going on?"

Malcolm hadn't been paying attention, and when he looked up, the red and blue lights made the van feel like some sort of disco. There were at least four police cars ahead of them, lights flashing, and then Malcolm noticed all the vans and cars with television station logos on them.

The visitor center was still off in the distance, surrounded by brightly colored trees showing their autumn plumage. The wooden building looked like a log cabin to Malcolm, but much bigger, with odd angles and a big sign that jutted up with the words "Parc Regional des Sept-Chutes" in huge lettering. The only way to approach the visitor's center was over a wooden bridge wide enough for one vehicle. A police car sat in the way, blocking anyone from walking in that direction.

"Oh boy, something's happening," Barry said as he turned off the engine. "Quick, get the cameras."

Malcolm helped pull out the main hand-held camera and handed it to Prisha. This was her expertise. His was just research, although he could handle the cameras if he had to. He then took the second camera, which was still screwed onto the tripod, and quickly undid it. He knew Barry would want both him and Prisha to record. It was always good to have a backup with a different angle, which would allow Prisha to do some editing to make it look more professional. Since they all wanted to impress the Discovery channel, this was a top priority.

Barry pushed his way through the crowd but stopped when he saw a film crew starting to pack up. "Excuse me," he said. "Does anyone know where we can find Sophie?"

A young reporter with a dark blue suit looked up and smiled the kind of smile that gets even mediocre people attention, especially media attention. "Sophie? The ranger?" he said. "She's off taking care of things and won't talk."

"What is this about?" Prisha asked.

"Another sighting," the reporter said. "And who are you? I thought I knew all the local media people."

Barry puffed up his chest. "We're the crew of 'Skeptic Soup' here to investigate. Surely, you've heard of us."

The reporter shook his head but kept his charismatic smile broad.

"We're about to sign a contract with the Discovery channel," Barry added. "We have many thousands of followers..."

"Oh, an internet thing," the reporter said. "Good for you."

Malcolm didn't like the kind way the reporter patronized them, so he stepped forward. "Another sighting? Another Gugwe sighting?"

"Yes," the reporter said, noticing Malcolm. "I'm sorry, where are my manners? I'm George Kaplan, with CHLT channel 7."

"A pleasure," Barry said. "I'm Barry Lowery and this is Malcolm Pulley and Prisha Singh. But, please, tell us about this sighting."

George smiled again, teeth shining in the morning sun. "We don't know much, other than a couple from Vermont was visiting and claim they saw the creature, too. We've interviewed them already, but Sophie has not made any public comment. That's what we were hoping for, but now they're saying there won't be any, so most of us here are packing up."

Prisha ran her fingers through her hair. "No one was hurt, were they?"

George raised his eyebrows. "No, we're lucky this time. Just a sighting in the distance, apparently."

"So who can we talk to about it?"

"No one right now," George said. "We won't get any details until Sophie is ready to release an official statement. If ever."

Barry thanked George, who held out his hand for everyone to shake. After that ceremony was completed, Barry headed toward the visitor center. At least half a dozen officers stood in their way, about twenty feet ahead. Malcolm tried to calculate how many meters that was and gave up. Barry stopped walking when he saw them all glaring at him.

"Mounties," Barry said.

"No, not Mounties," Prisha replied. "Just local police. Mounties are like, you know, Canada's version of the FBI or something, I think."

Malcolm grinned. "So we don't get to meet Dudley Do-Right?"

Barry ignored him. "Another sighting makes this story even better. But that's not unusual, is it? For there to be multiple sightings?"

"Not at all," Malcolm replied. "There are always copycat sightings. Sometimes it's just because this thing is fresh in everyone's mind, so when they see a shadow they can't identify, their mind fills in the missing pieces and then they're convinced it's something else—in this case, a Gugwe. And sometimes people lie for the attention."

Barry nodded his agreement. "And if this is a scam like I think it is—just some guy in a suit trying to scare kids and tourists—then it makes sense the scammer may do this a second time to make the first sighting more believable."

"Or else the Gugwe is real," Prisha said.

Barry's mouth tightened. "Oh, don't be ridiculous."

"Well, what if it's that big thing that Malcolm talked about that the scientists thought was extinct? You never know."

"We're supposed to be the skeptics," Barry said.

Prisha shook her head. "A kid is still missing."

Malcolm continued filming the police standing before the visitor's center. The footage could be good background images when editing the final story together. The officers stood at attention and tried to look really important and serious. "We're also supposed to think like scientists and look for evidence. And if the evidence indicates that there is a creature out there, then we shouldn't discount it." He stopped filming and held the camera to his side, and the officers went back to their normal relaxed poses, talking to each other. "I mean, this isn't the kind of thing we usually do, where we're disproving ghosts or people who claim to have ESP or something that defies the laws of nature. This thing could exist without being supernatural in the slightest."

"Yes. Well." Barry looked like he was having trouble responding. "We're not scientists."

"I am," Malcolm said.

"You're a *political* scientist!" Barry growled. "You have a worthless degree in *political* science! That's not the same thing."

Malcolm gave Barry a huge grin. Barry rolled his eyes in response.

"Look over there," Prisha quietly said, nodding her head toward an area under a tree where a young woman sat at a picnic table. "A ranger."

"Maybe that's Sophie," Malcolm said.

"Doubtful," Barry replied. "But maybe she'll talk." He began a brisk pace in that direction as Malcolm and Prisha trotted to catch up.

The ranger raised her head as they approached and then stood, hands held behind her back. She gave them a suspicious look but maintained her professional face. Malcolm realized that they didn't look much like journalists, with their blue jeans and zip-up jackets. The ranger probably assumed they were just tourists who shouldn't be here. She held her hand up and said something in French.

"I'm so sorry," Prisha said, taking big steps to keep up with Barry. "My French is very poor, but I think you said we are in the wrong place?"

The ranger looked a bit frustrated, and Malcolm imagined her thinking 'Stupid Americans,' but that look lasted but a second. "I do not think you are supposed to be here," she said. "May I help you?"

"Yes, thank you," Barry said, coming to a stop about ten feet before the ranger. "We're with … the Discovery channel, and we're doing a documentary on the Gugwe." He paused. "I'm sorry. I don't mean to… that is… we're doing a documentary *for* the Discovery channel, but they haven't officially accepted it yet."

Malcolm smiled. Barry might be hard to get along with, but he was unfailingly honest and a terrible liar. Malcolm wasn't sure if it was some inner conscience that made him that way, or his need to be believed. After all, if the whole point of Skeptic Soup was to expose frauds and "fake news" about the supernatural, it wouldn't do if the person doing the exposure was seen as dishonest.

The ranger's face was unreadable. She remained silent.

"Anyway," Barry said. "We had an appointment with Sophie, but she's clearly too busy right now. Could we possibly ask you a few questions?"

The ranger smiled. "I do not have the... the authority to make official statements." She looked concerned, as if she wasn't sure that was the correct English word.

"Oh, it doesn't have to be official," Prisha said, stepping forward. "We won't even record it if you want. We just want to know what is going on."

"I do not know much..."

"You certainly know more than we do, at least," Prisha said. "I'm sorry, where are my manners? I am Prisha Singh, and this is Malcolm Pulley and Barry Lowery."

"A pleasure," the ranger said. "I am Ranger Gagnon."

"Thank you," Prisha said, smiling broadly. "We do have a YouTube channel with hundreds of thousands of viewers, so it's not like we're just tourists. Can you please just tell us what is happening? We heard that someone else saw the Gugwe."

"Maybe."

Malcolm glanced at Barry, impressed that he was remaining silent and letting Prisha handle this. Perhaps he saw that her personality and her professional attire was indeed better suited for interviewing friendly witnesses.

"Yes, of course, they could have been mistaken," Prisha said. "Did they describe it? Where did they see it?"

"I am not certain where they claim to see it," Ranger Gagnon said. "I am not the person in charge of that. I do know that they were scared, and it did not look like they were lying. But I know we have black bears here..."

"Exactly, that's what we thought," Barry said. "Especially after a recent alleged sighting of the creature—that could be in the minds of others so that when they see a bear, they imagine something else."

Ranger Gagnon looked at Barry and then gave a slight shrug. "Maybe."

Prisha raised an eyebrow. "Have you ever seen the Gugwe?"

Ranger Gagnon's eyes widened, and she looked at each in turn. "Maybe," she repeated.

Prisha clapped her hands. "Wonderful! As you know, we're researching it and want to find out as much as we can. When did you see... something that maybe could have been the Gugwe?"

The ranger looked around. There was no one else near. "I was just a little girl. It was on the bord of the woods... Bord?" She moved her hands in a cutting fashion.

"Edge?" Malcolm said.

"Yes, edge of woods. I screamed; I was so scared. My parents told me it was just a bear, but even as a little girl, I know what a bear is. This? Not a bear."

Prisha sat next to the ranger. "Was that near here?"

Ranger Gagnon shook her head. "No, about twenty kilometers away. I never saw it again." Her intense stare made Prisha lean away. "Except in dreams."

The seriousness of her statement made everyone quiet for a few seconds. No one wanted to ask a follow-up question.

The silence was short-lived.

"There you are!"

Malcolm spun around. A stocky police officer with an angry expression pointed at them while pacing steadily and determinedly in their direction. Malcolm marveled at how he looked just like the stereotype of an American officer, with dark sunglasses, a '70s mustache, and a grim expression that signaled inexperience with smiling. A younger, smaller version of himself paced alongside, although with a clean-shaven face.

Prisha was the first to recover. "Good afternoon, officers. We're…"

"I know who you are," the big one growled. "You're those podcast skeptics." His English was quite good, but his French accent pushed at the words, trying to escape. "You've been bothering our people."

Barry stepped forward and held out his hand. "I'm so glad you have heard of us, and obviously know of our reputation for serious journalism. But I don't think we have bothered anyone. Why, the people we have talked to have been most accommodating and friendly…"

The officer scowled, refused to shake Barry's hand, and nodded his head. "Like Ranger Gagnon here?"

"I could have refused to speak to them," Ranger Gagnon said. "They weren't bothering me, Captain Picard."

"Captain Picard?" Barry smiled. "That's your name? Captain Picard?"

Picard stepped forward and glared at Barry. "You think it's funny? You think there are no real people with that last name?"

Malcolm realized why the man was so grumpy. He must have gotten teased a lot when he was younger, and then to actually become a captain…

Barry calmed himself immediately. "No, sir. Please accept my apologies. We've just dealt with people who run scams and such, and often they use fake names, so I reacted inappropriately to this very real situation."

Picard stared at him for a few seconds and then pointed an angry finger at Barry's chest. "You're not supposed to be here. If you've done your homework, you'd know that the park has been closed to everyone ever since the disappearance, and that's not about to change any time soon. I know you're doing one of your silly podcasts, but we don't need you interfering and getting in the way of our investigation, yes?"

"We would never get in the way of officers doing their duty," Barry said. "But perhaps you would be willing to be interviewed for our show? Having the captain in charge of the investigation would be a great treat for our viewers."

"Not to mention that you obviously know more than anyone about what is going on!" Prisha said, batting her eyes and smiling broadly. "And we can see that other reporters have been allowed to stay and talk. Can we ask you about—"

"No, you cannot. You are not reporters. You're kids with a YouTube channel. Even my nephew has one of those. He talks about video games or something and has tons of followers." He crossed his arms. "Leave now or I'll have you arrested for trespassing."

Barry looked shocked. "Trespassing? But we—"

"This is not a negotiation. You will get back in your van, leave, and stop coming to the park until it is open again, which probably won't be until after you have gone back to the States." He then mumbled, "Especially if I have any say in the matter."

"We can help your investigation!" Barry said, holding out his hands. "We have information that you might want. Let us tell you what we've found out about—"

"Now."

"But surely, you understand that we're only trying to help—"

"Sergeant," Picard said, motioning to his assistant. "Please arrest these trespassers."

As they rode in the back of the police van to the magistrate's office, Malcolm wondered if maybe becoming a captain was something Picard had aimed for his entire life solely so he could abuse people who laughed at his name.

CHAPTER FIVE

The handcuffs didn't bother Malcolm as much as having to listen to Barry talk about how his rights were being violated and how the American embassy would hear of this and how he was a famous internet star who would expose this blatant example of corruption. Prisha tried her best to calm him down, and eventually tried telling him to just shut it, but finally gave up and just sat in silence.

The police station was tiny, nestled in a wooded area with only small convenience store nearby. Picard escorted them into a windowless waiting room. A large mirror on one wall broke the monotony. Fluorescent lights bathed the room in a soft-white glow. A table with four chairs looked to be bolted to the floor, and there were bars at the bottom of the chairs, clearly for the purpose of attaching ankle cuffs to prevent their guests from escaping.

Picard left the room as his assistant removed their handcuffs, smiled at them, and then shut the door.

Malcolm rubbed his wrists. "You'd think they'd put some sort of padding on these things."

Barry scoffed. "Yeah, if there is one thing police want, it's to make their prisoners comfortable."

Prisha stretched and sat on one of the hard, plastic chairs. After glancing around the room, she leaned forward and whispered, "I'm sure we're being watched through that two-way mirror, and they're probably listening in as well."

Barry nodded. "It's not like we have anything to hide."

"I think they're just trying to scare us," Malcom replied quietly. "I mean, they've treated us fairly well, considering. They let us store our equipment in the van first and everything."

Prisha shrugged. "Well, they're Canadians."

"It's a way to get us to agree with them," Barry said, voice low. "They're playing 'good cop, bad cop' here. That other cop was the one who allowed us to store the equipment, and you notice that he's the one who took our cuffs off."

Malcolm shrugged, then gave Barry a serious look. Barry returned a slow nod. Malcolm sat back in his chair, tilted his head back until he was staring at the ceiling, then said loud enough for everyone to hear, "So what do we do now? If we can't check out the park, we can't. We can still interview people, I guess."

Prisha nodded her agreement. "I'd say we've pretty much done all we can at this point. We probably should just head back home and file our report with whatever we have."

Barry pouted, sat down heavily, and ran his hands through his hair. "Yeah, this isn't going too well. Damn it, I thought we were close. But I guess you're right. Plus, our budget is running out. We should probably just stick with what we know how to do best. There's plenty of stuff on the web we can use for reference to do our story. We don't have to actually be here for that."

They remained silent in their own thoughts for at least another ten minutes before Picard came back into the room. "Follow me," he said. "The judge will see you."

A short walk down the hallway led to another small room where a large television was mounted on the wall. Picard motioned to three chairs facing the television, and everyone sat quietly. He then grabbed a remote, clicked it a few times, and the screen came on. A middle-aged woman with large round glasses appeared, clearly adjusting her own monitor. Her mouth moved a bit, and then she held up a hand and stared down before doing something off-screen. After a few moments, she looked up and said some words in French. Picard answered her similarly, and the two spoke for a few sentences before Barry said, "I'm sorry, but if you're talking about us, can you please speak in English?"

Picard glared at him. "I'm just letting the judge know what is going on and why you are here."

Barry crossed his arms. "I would think that even in Canada, the defendant is allowed to participate in his own hearing."

The judge nodded. "It was only preliminary matters, nothing serious," she said, with a fairly strong accent. "I apologize for not being there in person, but since Covid, we've found that doing it by Zoom is much easier, especially since my courthouse is about an hour's drive away. Anyway, I am told that you were arrested for trespassing at the park."

"Yes, may I address that?" Barry asked.

"Let me get some housekeeping done first," the judge said. "I am Magistrate Marie Bellanger and I have to ask some questions." The next few minutes were spent providing names, addresses, and other information needed for the court's paperwork. When it was concluded, the judge sat back in her padded seat and clasped her hands together. "Captain, these people have not yet been charged, no?"

"Not yet," Picard said. "I wanted to bring them to you first."

"A bit unusual, but yes, tell me what this is about."

Picard cleared his throat and then began. "They are not journalists, but—"

"Hey!" Barry said. "I mean, objection! We certainly are—"

"You will have your turn, Mr. Lowery," Judge Bellanger said. "Allow the captain to continue, and then you may respond. Captain, be brief, please."

Picard unsuccessfully hid a grin. "They were at the park when it was closed to the public and when asked to leave, they refused to do so. I took them in for trespassing. I am investigating as well whether they should be charged with harassing our citizens."

Judge Bellanger nodded. "Very well. Mr. Lowery, you may now speak."

Barry took a breath, and to Malcolm's pleasure, remained calm. "We *are* journalists. We may not write for old-fashioned newspapers or perform for television news, but we have a very large internet presence, with many followers, and if all goes well, will soon have our own show on the Discovery channel. I point this out because often, people refuse to acknowledge that we are indeed journalists, but the world has changed and—"

"Yes, I understand," the judge said. "Why is all that relevant?"

"Because there were other journalists there and they were not charged with trespassing," Barry said. "You are discriminating against us in a way that clearly violates our first amendment rights."

"Barry, this is Canada," Malcolm said. "They don't have a first amendment."

Barry waved a dismissing hand. "The same principle applies."

Judge Bellanger tilted her head. "What is the name of your internet thing?"

"It's a show called 'Skeptic Soup' where we investigate hard-to-believe things." Barry pursed his lips. "If we find out something is true even though we initially believed it wasn't, we'll report that. We're after the truth."

"Why 'soup'?"

"It's memorable and it flows nicely," Barry said, having been asked that question many times before. "You remembered it, didn't you? That's the most important thing."

"I remembered because you said it only two seconds before."

Prisha leaned forward. "We use the metaphor of having a bunch of ingredients mixed together like in a soup — those are the facts — and our job is to figure out what the ingredients are to determine what the final truth is. What the soup is. What kind of soup it is. If it's even soup." She sounded less convinced of her words the more she talked, so she finally sat back, head low and eyes looking up at the judge on the screen.

Judge Bellanger's expression changed from skeptical to amused. "That's stretching a metaphor pretty far."

"We thought of the metaphor after we thought of the name," Barry admitted. "It may not have been our most coherent decision."

Picard gave a small cough. "If I may, Your Honor, I think they should at least be ordered to stop harassing our citizens."

Barry turned to face the officer. "Harassing? Every single person we've interviewed agreed to the interview. We've harassed no one."

"They are here specifically to make fun of anyone who has claimed to see the Gugwe!" Picard said. "All their show does is try to debunk things and make believers look foolish."

"That's not so!" Prisha leaned forward. "Like I said, we're here to find out the truth. Often, the truth is that people create scams and lie about things, but if the Gugwe is real, you know, we want to find out and we'll report it!" She glared at Picard. "A boy is missing, and his friend is worried and was very believable. We've spoken to others who also have seen the creature, and even if we don't find evidence of it, we can't rule out that it's not real."

Judge Bellanger raised an eyebrow. "Your purpose is not just to report?"

"We're investigative journalists, Your Honor," Barry said. "But we can do that anywhere, honestly. We don't have to be at the site of the disappearance to do that. We want to find out of the Gugwe is real, given how many people have claimed to have seen it over the years."

The judge took a long minute looking at everyone, and then spoke. "Captain, if the park is closed to everyone, why were journalists there?"

Picard shifted his feet and didn't look at the screen for a few seconds before answering. "Um, well, there was another sighting, and the rangers thought it would be best to let the journalists into the parking lot area at least so they'd have a good image for the cameras and everything. I mean, they were going to do the story whether we helped or not, so might as well be accommodating. But no one was allowed past the parking lot, and now that they've done their piece, they're not allowed back."

Judge Bellanger nodded. "Fine. I don't believe you have probable cause to arrest these three, and I think they understand now that they should not be at the park, no? Nor should they harass anyone, although I have heard no evidence to support that accusation." She then addressed the trio. "I don't expect to see you again, yes? You will obey the police and leave if they ask you to. You do not need to be at the park."

Barry nodded. "Yes, we do not need to be at the park."

She smiled. "Very good. Treat this as a warning. If I see you again, it may not be as nice, no? Captain, you can drive them back to their van."

Barry smiled. "Yes, Picard, make it so."

Picard rolled his eyes. "Oh, my, no one has ever made that joke to me before." He waved them out of the room, and had his unnamed assistant drive them back to their van.

The assistant said very little during the trip. Malcolm wondered if he just didn't speak English other than small phrases like "This way" and "Goodbye."

Once in their van and driving back to the motel, Barry spoke. "Do you think that worked?"

Malcolm shrugged. "The fact that we pretended we were going to give up and leave may have at least convinced the judge to let us go."

"Picard probably was listening in and told the judge before we got there," Prisha said. "So yeah, you know, it may have helped."

Malcolm rubbed his wrists. "We should have told him about Nathan's hiding place."

"We tried, remember? He kept cutting us off. So it's his fault." Barry crossed his arms. "Besides, now we have a chance to go there first and film an exclusive."

"Didn't you promise we wouldn't go there again?"

"No." Barry smiled. "I agreed that we didn't *need* to be in the park. I never said we wouldn't go there anyway." He turned into the motel's parking lot. "It will be easier to sneak in if we go at night."

"Also easier to get lost and easier to get attacked by a bear," Malcolm said. "Or a Gugwe. Barry, did you bring a gun, just in case?"

Barry shut off the engine. "A *gun*? You think I own a gun? Have you ever seen me with a gun? Don't you know my position on gun control?" He unstrapped his seat belt and turned to face Malcolm in the back seat. "Anyway, they'd never let us across the border with a weapon."

Malcolm nodded. "I guess," he said. "I just don't like wandering through strange woods unprotected."

"*There is no Gugwe!*" Barry said. "Those kids probably snuck up there at night all the time without any problem. I'm sure we'll be fine."

Malcolm unstrapped his seat belt and didn't meet Barry's eyes. He did not share his fellow's confidence.

CHAPTER SIX

Malcolm stared at his phone, reading up on Gugwe sightings. A rest before nightfall was appreciated, and he cuddled his head into his pillow while lying on top of the sheets. Barry sat at the small desk the motel provided, laptop before him. "Our numbers aren't doing that well this week," he reported.

"We haven't posted anything in a while. Prisha hasn't even had a spare moment to edit the preview video." Malcolm stretched out and placed his phone down. "Are you sure it's a good idea to go check out Nathan's campsite tonight?"

Barry spun around in the small office chair and continued to twist in circles, as if that would help him concentrate. "If we don't, Nathan's mother will tell Picard, who will go there first, block it off, and then we'd never get the story we want. She may have already done that and it may already be too late."

"I suppose. But I sure don't want to be arrested again."

"Don't worry, they're not going to—"

A knock on the door caused both to sit up straight, startled. Malcolm opened his eyes wide to Barry, who waved him toward the door. *Oh sure*, Malcolm thought. *Let me be the first one arrested.* He twisted himself out of bed and went to the door slowly. As he leaned forward to peek through the keyhole, he heard Prisha's voice outside.

"Open up already, you idiots."

Malcolm pulled open the door and she burst in. "You know that couple that saw the Gugwe? I just saw them on the local news, and they're staying right here in this motel!"

Barry jumped out of his seat. "What?"

"Seriously, while we were being arrested, they must have come back here, you know, and then the press found out and came here and interviewed them. They're probably still here."

"What luck!" Barry grabbed his shoes and sat back down, quickly slipping them on and tying them. "Get the portable camera. Let's see if we can find them."

A few minutes later, the trio entered the lobby — or what served as a lobby for this small hotel. A desk for the manager, a few old sofas spread out for guests, a table with a microwave and an old coffee maker, and a vending machine selling sodas and potato chips.

On the sofa, regaling their tale, were the two from the TV show. The manager and a few others staying there were listening in and asking questions. The couples' faces clearly showed how much they were enjoying the attention.

"Oh, yeah," Barry mumbled. "We're not going to have any problem getting these guys to talk."

Prisha turned on the light attached to the camera, which instantly got everyone's attention. Barry jumped in.

"Hello, I'm Barry Lowery, and I'm wondering if we could have a few words about your experience for our show?"

The first fellow beamed with excitement. "Yes, of course! Just tell us what to do." The other sat up straighter and tried to slick back unruly hair.

Barry motioned for Prisha to start recording while Malcolm pulled out his phone to record backup. "Thank you so much," Barry said. "Can we have your names?"

"I'm David Adams and this is Josh Friedman." David smiled broadly for the camera. "I'm not sure what we could tell you that we haven't already told everyone else."

"Nevertheless, our viewers would like to hear it straight from you. So you're visiting tourists, I understand?"

"From Vermont," Josh said. "Going to visit friends in Quebec City but taking our time and seeing the sights."

"Ah, we're from Boston," Barry said. "But we love visiting Vermont. Beautiful in the fall, especially around Burlington."

"That's where we're from," David said. "We really like it there."

Malcolm gave a sigh as he looked at his phone to assure he was getting everyone in the picture. These opening bits were normally important for the interviewee to feel comfortable, but in this case, they seemed unnecessary. These two were loving the attention and didn't need any warming up.

"So tell me," Barry said, "about what you saw. When and where did this happen?"

Josh spread his arms. "It was early this morning, around ten or so—"

"Oh no, it wasn't," David said. "It was almost lunch."

"It doesn't matter." Josh waved David's objection away. "It was still morning, that's all. Sun was out at the time—not cloudy like now—and we were walking on the trail toward the largest waterfall."

"No one else around," David added.

"Yes, and then there's this small hill where there's no trees because it's so steep or something, and we looked up, and there it was, at the top of the hill."

"Very good," Barry said. "A daytime sighting. How far away were you?"

"I dunno," David said. "Maybe forty feet?"

"More or less," Josh said.

"Thank you for not using meters," Barry said with a grin. "So what did it look like?"

Both men stumbled over each other's words to describe it.

"Big, hairy…"

"Standing upright…"

"Ape-like but dog-like, too…"

"Holding on to a branch, looking down at us…"

"Smelly…"

"Smelly? I didn't smell anything."

"Well, did you remember to take your sinus pill this morning?"

"Even if I had, and I did, I don't ever remember you mentioning smell before."

"Very good," Barry interrupted. "Had either of you ever heard of this creature before today?"

David smiled. "Sure. Well, not until we got here. We saw the news about the missing boy, and saw some of the tourist things…"

"There's a bumper sticker that says, 'I visited the Gugwe at Les Sept-Chutes'," Josh said. "I suppose we should get that now."

Barry leaned closer. "So you saw the creature for how long?"

"Oh, just seconds," Josh said. "Then it jumped back into the woods."

"Can you be certain it wasn't a bear? Or just a really big guy in a hairy coat?"

"Pretty certain," David said. "It left a chill in me when I saw it. I mean, it was so unexpected."

"And weird." Josh nodded enthusiastically.

"Well, let's suppose you had never heard of this creature before," Barry said. "What would you think it was?"

"Well, I think I would have said Bigfoot," David replied after a second's thought. "I mean, I've heard of Bigfoot. Except it wasn't Bigfoot like in those pictures. It was standing upright pretty good."

Barry pressed on. "Do you think the fact that people are talking about the Gugwe may have influenced your opinion of what you saw?"

"No, I know what we saw," David said. He jutted out his jaw. "Don't you believe us?"

"I certainly have no reason to doubt you saw something," Barry said. "But we just need to confirm what it was. You didn't take a picture—"

"It happened too quick."

"—and the chances of you being mistaken are there, after all."

"Mistaken!" Josh sat back. "Well, I suppose that's better than calling us liars."

David pointed a finger at Barry. "What show did you say you were from?"

"It's a YouTube show that may soon be on the Discovery channel," Barry said. "It's called 'Skeptic Soup.'"

"Skeptics!" David looked like he wanted to spit. "You should have told us that to begin with. Come on, Josh." He stood up and walked out, making it a point not to make eye contact with anyone.

Josh followed behind. "What a stupid name for a show," he said.

The other people gathered around looked uncomfortable, and also rose and went back to whatever business they were doing before, while trying to stay out of the camera's range.

Prisha filmed the couple walking out the door, and then turned off the camera and the light. She nodded for Malcolm and Barry to follow her, and they went down the hallway to their rooms.

"I think Malcolm's comment about copycat viewers fits here," Barry said as they entered their room. "We can certainly use that. Points to the hysteria that often comes with these sightings."

"And they were, you know, miles away from where Nathan described his hiding spot," Prisha said.

Malcolm shrugged. "Well, those things could easily travel for miles."

"Not here." Barry grinned. "They'd have to travel for kilometers."

Malcolm ignored him while Prisha groaned.

Barry smiled, pleased with the reaction. "Okay, everyone get a few hours or so of rest and then we'll head up to Nathan's place once it's dark."

"Sounds like a seedy bar," Prisha said. "'Nathan's Place—no Gugwes allowed.'"

CHAPTER SEVEN

Barry stuffed the flashlight into the backpack. "Do we have everything?"

"I still say this is a bad idea." Malcolm checked to make sure his phone was charged. "We've had a crazy busy day, we've hardly rested, it's late at night, and the police may still be there at the park."

Barry sat on the bed. "Look, I understand all that. But we have to be practical, here." He stuffed a sweater into his backpack. "First, we really are on a budget and the longer we stay here, the more in debt we go. Second, they think we plan on leaving so they'll probably not even be paying attention to us. And third, even if they do, they won't think we're bold enough to go there the same night we were arrested."

"I need more coffee," Prisha said. "And not this terrible motel crap." She glared angrily at the Keurig machine and its pods of generic coffee. "We really should bring our own coffeemaker with us on these trips, especially when we're going who-knows-where."

"Ooh, good idea." Malcolm went to his suitcase and pulled out a hoodie to add to his backpack. Barry was right—it would probably get cold in the mountains at night. Prisha, meanwhile, had come to their room with her bag packed and with a fluffy coat already on. "Or at least we should bring our own coffee pods for the machine."

"Not all motels have coffee machines, you know," Prisha said. "We need our own."

"Can we stop talking about coffee?" Barry crossed his arms. "Although, yeah, I could use one, too. We don't want to fall asleep or not be completely aware when we go to investigate. There must be someplace around here…" He pulled out his phone and started tapping while Malcolm packed the main camera into his bag, along with another flashlight. "Okay, fine, the Tim Horton's is still open."

Malcolm smiled "More donuts!"

Barry picked up his backpack and slung it over his shoulder. "Fine, coffee and donuts and then to the park. The sooner we get our story, the sooner we can get back home."

Barry led the way as they left the motel and walked to the van. The stars were hidden by dark clouds and Malcolm hoped that didn't mean more rain was on the way. He opened the back of the van, and they placed their backpacks behind the back seat. Malcolm checked to make sure the main camera was secure in its bag and then opened the rear door and settled into his normal spot. He preferred not riding shotgun. Sitting in the back allowed him to look at his phone, read a book, or otherwise stay out of Barry's way. Malcolm preferred being lost in his own thoughts to making small talk, anyway. Besides, Prisha liked being up front and being Barry's navigator, despite the GPS.

Everyone strapped in and Barry started the engine. After a pitstop to stock up on coffee and donuts, he drove toward the park. "We can't go to the main entrance," he said. "Prisha, I asked you to find a good spot for us to park."

"I know," she said. "To get to the kids' camp area like they described, we'll have to park about a half a mile away at that dirt road Nathan mentioned, you know, and then go through the woods until we reach the trail."

Malcolm coughed. "At night, with no moon. Great."

"Did you check the forecast for rain?" Prisha asked.

"Yeah." Malcolm glanced out the window. "Although that sky certainly doesn't look like ten percent chance to me."

Barry turned onto the main road. "We need to do this tonight. Besides, during the day, we're much more likely to get caught."

"But much less likely to run into a bear," Malcolm said.

"Or a Gugwe," added Prisha.

Barry sighed. "There is no Gugwe."

"You keep saying that, but you know it's possible," Prisha said. "I think you're expecting a Scooby Doo moment, where we find some guy in a gorilla suit, pull off his mask, and have him say he would have gotten away with it had it not been for us meddling kids."

Barry snorted. "That's much more likely than finding out that some ancient creature has remained hidden for thousands of years without being discovered."

"It's probably just a bear." Malcolm yawned. "People see it for a few seconds and their mind fills in the blanks and the next thing you know, they all think it's some monster."

Barry nodded. "There's plenty of scientific evidence for that phenomenon."

Prisha pointed. "Turn there."

Barry slowed down the van. "That's a road? It's more like a path."

"Well, that's what the Google map showed." She stared at her phone. "Looks like some sort of maintenance road."

"Not even paved."

Prisha looked up. "At least we can pull off the paved road a bit, you know, so no one can see us. Then we can walk from there."

A small curve took them out of sight of the main road, and Barry stopped the van.

"What?" Malcolm asked from the back seat. "Are we there already?"

"No, there's a barrier."

Malcolm leaned forward, peered between the front seats, and saw that the road was blocked with a gate with a large sign shining in the headlights.

"No trespassing," he read.

As he unstrapped his seat belt, Barry said over his shoulder, "Let's see if it's locked." He climbed out with the van still running and walked to the metal barrier and then leaned down to read the sign.

"Smaller printing underneath," he reported. "'Warning. Bears in the area. Closed to hikers and campers.'"

Walking to the edge, he popped the gate, and it swung open. "Guess they figured they didn't need to lock it," he said.

"Canadians," Prisha mumbled.

Barry came back and shut off the engine, causing Malcolm to flinch. "Wait, we're still going to go?" he asked. "With bears? Those signs aren't there for nothing."

"The kids went up there all the time," Barry said. "I'm sure it's safe."

Malcolm grumbled under his breath as the packs were unloaded, flashlights were engaged, and sweaters and hoodies were slipped on. Soon, all three stood ready, staring at each other.

"Spooky," Malcolm said.

Prisha grinned. "My make-up, or the starless, cloudy, autumn night?"

"Okay, goth girl." Barry scanned the area with his flashlight. "We follow this road a bit. Then what?"

"We look for the boob rocks." She giggled. "Apparently they're made of silicone."

"A natural substance often found in rocks." Malcolm grinned, anxious to be thinking of anything except bears. He started walking. "I understand that it's a great place to find a titmouse."

Prisha took up beside him. "I think you can also find them near a Hooter's."

"Well, I see you're keeping abreast of the situation."

Barry strapped his flashlight to his belt, which allowed his hands to be free. "Sorry, I can't think of any bad boob puns at the moment. But do please go on." He winked at the two and walked with strong, even paces to place himself in the front.

Malcolm didn't care—Barry could get eaten by the bear first, giving Malcolm time to run away. He then immediately felt guilty for thinking that.

He instead turned his thoughts to his surroundings. The night seemed fairly normal, other than being overcast and dark. But what did Malcolm know? He had spent most of his life in Brooklyn before moving to Boston for college. In Brooklyn, the closest one got to "woods" was Prospect Park. He had never even been camping and hated the thought of having to sleep in a tent or use a latrine.

He licked his lips, and wondered if the noises around him were normal. Crickets chirped and frogs bellowed and there were other sounds that he couldn't identify. But at least there were sounds. Animals got quiet when something dangerous was nearby, right? The background noise of running water seemed to be coming from everywhere. A cold breeze wafted over them every few minutes, chilling him momentarily, carrying the strong smells of the trees and plants and, in the distance, the spray of a waterfall. He glanced at Barry and Prisha, but they seemed perfectly accepting of their surroundings. That gave Malcolm a bit of comfort. But not much.

He kept pace and then realized that quite a few minutes had gone by with everyone silent, lost in their own thoughts.

"You know, I still haven't had time to update our social media," Prisha said. "Usually, we post a teaser every few days or so on Instagram and Facebook and such. I should at least post some clips from my interview with that kid."

"Well, we're going to do some filming tonight, of course," Barry said. He pushed aside a branch blocking the road and then held it aside for Prisha and Malcolm to pass through. "You can use some of that tomorrow."

"Bad idea," Malcolm said. "We need to save any clips of us here until after we're back in the States."

"Oh, right." Barry nodded his agreement. "No need to piss off Picard."

Prisha giggled again. "We'd be hoisted on our own picard."

Barry laughed. "What is with you and terrible puns tonight?"

"Lack of sleep, probably. Need more coffee."

"Look!" Malcolm pointed with his flashlight. "Boobs!"

The other two flung their beams in the direction Malcolm indicated and sure enough, two large boulders blocked any view of the woods beyond. Set back about twenty feet from the road, they could easily be missed by anyone driving by. "I almost missed them," Malcolm said. "We could have kept walking for hours."

"I don't know." Prisha placed her hands on her hips. "They don't look like boobs to me."

Barry began walking toward the boulders, pushing weeds out of his path. "To a hormonal teenage boy, everything looks like boobs. Come on, if these aren't the right rocks, we can get back on the road."

"Didn't Nathan say there was a hidden path behind them?" Malcolm followed behind, shining his light to the sides of the boulders. "Like a ditch? If we don't find one, we'll know."

Barry nodded but didn't respond. He walked around the rocks and Malcolm and Prisha could see the flashlight beam spinning in all directions. As they joined him, Barry was pulling the flashlight off his belt so as to better guide it.

"Is that a path?" he asked.

Malcolm squinted as he pointed his beam at the ground. "Hard to tell in the darkness, but I think so."

Barry hefted his backpack and began walking. "Well, there's no other path, so let's see where this takes us."

Malcolm and Prisha followed, their flashlights moving back and forth with their paces.

"Maybe we shouldn't be talking or making so much noise," Malcom said. "Won't that attract animals?"

"Nah." Barry looked back over his shoulder. "If anything, it will scare them away. Unusual lights and voices are how they keep animals away from things."

"And the animals here are used to humans," Prisha added. "It's, you know, a public park, after all. They know to stay clear."

"Well, it didn't scare away whatever it was that chased the kids," Malcolm said. "And that wasn't even at night."

"Don't worry, city boy," Barry said. "I used to be a boy scout. Almost made Eagle, too, but then high school started, and the drama club had girls."

"What do you expect to find once we get there?" Prisha asked, cutting off Barry's high school memories. "What can we possibly find that the police haven't already found?"

"We don't even know if the police have been there yet," Malcolm replied. "Remember, Nathan's mom was going to have him tell the police but then we said we would. She may have already told them but maybe not. And we tried to tell the police, but Picard cut us off, you know, so that's not our fault. We may beat the police there."

"Aha!" Barry said. "Now aren't you glad I decided to go tonight?"

Prisha blew a raspberry. "You didn't even know that fact when you decided to go tonight, you know."

"But it's still another good reason, nonetheless!"

Barry picked up the pace. Malcolm tried to follow, but the footing was uneven in many places, with roots and forest debris covering the hilly path. The sound of running water grew louder. And he kept hearing movement in the woods. Squirrels? At night? Or wolves? Were there wolves there? Or bears? There's definitely bears there. Everyone said that.

"So tell me about this extinct gorilla thing," Prisha said after a few more minutes.

"Oh, sure." Malcolm was glad to have something to take his mind off the bears. "Um. It's the *Arctodus simus*. There are skeletons of it in museums. Lived like twelve thousand years ago. It's also called the 'giant, short-faced bear,' which is why I thought of the Gugwe descriptions. It went extinct in the Quaternary extinction event."

"The what what?" Barry asked, without looking back.

"The Quaternary extinction event. That's where lots of creatures went extinct, probably due to climactic changes combined with human hunting."

"But you, you know, think maybe some survived." Prisha raised an eyebrow.

"No, that would be impossible," Malcolm said. "I mean, hardly anyone has ever claimed to have seen one in the twelve thousand years since then. If it was still around, you'd think there would be more sightings, right? It's just fun to speculate, that's all. I'm sure those kids just saw a bear and, like Bigfoot and other such things, they misidentified it in a way that made their memories give them a better story."

"Exactly," Barry said. "My thoughts exactly. Glad to hear you don't believe—"

"But I'm open to facts," Malcolm said. "If there is evidence of this thing still existing, wouldn't that be amazing? That would be so cool."

"Until they kill your friends."

Malcolm took a deep breath. The roar of the waterfall was becoming overbearing, and he had to speak louder to be heard. "We don't know whether that kid is dead or just missing or ran away..." He let his sentence hang in the air as everyone was once more lost in their thoughts.

Barry pushed aside some brush and then stopped. "Well, lookie here. I think we found our secret campsite."

Chapter Eight

The area had been cleared with the leaves and other forest debris pushed to the edges of the camp. A rusty rake leaned against a tree, brown leaves trapped in its prongs. Three thick logs were arranged in the center to provide seating before what normally would have been a campfire but instead was replaced by an old, worn Transformer toy in the middle. A thick rope with knots every few feet hung from a sturdy branch near the edge of the clearing.

It was obvious that the place had not been kept up for the last week or so, because while the campsite was obvious, new, colorful leaves decorated the clearing, waiting for the kids to once more rake them out of the way.

Malcolm aimed his flashlight into the tree branches and discovered a make-shift tree fort composed of old boards nestled between strong branches. A green tarp hung suspended over the platform by thin ropes to provide protection against the rain.

"Pretty cool," Prisha said. "Some kids in my neighborhood did something like this in the woods behind their house when I was young. They used to have a rope like that, too, and we'd swing on it and fling ourselves into a pile of leaves."

Barry paced around, moving the light's beam back and forth, but saying nothing.

"Are there footprints anywhere?" Malcolm asked. "Maybe we can see if there are bear prints."

"Or Bigfoot?" Prisha said, pointing her light to the ground. "The ground here is soft…"

"Maybe there's a clue in the treehouse," Malcolm said, walking toward the rope. "Prisha, can you shine the light for me so I can see?"

"You just want to play in the fort," she said, pointing her beam in that direction.

Malcolm grinned, strapped his flashlight to his belt, and began climbing the rope. He easily stepped onto the platform but had to duck to get under the tarp. "Not too sturdy," he announced while pulling out his light.

He had to crawl, because standing in that small spot was impossible. Looking around revealed that there was nothing of interest there. The platform looked big enough to hold maybe two people tightly but that was it.

"Perhaps that was their lookout to see if anyone was coming," Prisha said.

"I suppose," Malcolm said, as he crawled back to the rope. "Then again, this bong under a blanket may indicate otherwise. There's always—"

Barry let out a cry.

"What?" Prisha said at the same time Malcolm cried back, "What is it?"

"Nothing," Barry said. "I… I thought I saw something."

Malcolm hurried down the rope and ran to where Barry stood at the edge of the camp. Prisha was already there, her flashlight beam scouring the area where Barry was looking.

Barry tried to regain his composure. "I think perhaps the stories have me seeing things," he said. "I thought I saw two eyes in the woods as my beam went past, but when I moved it back, they weren't there."

Prisha looked at him. "I'm sure there are lots of animals here," she said. "Could have been, you know, a raccoon or something."

"Too tall," Barry said. "If I wasn't imagining it, it was too tall. Could have been a bear." He continued to peer into the darkness.

They all remained still and silent, moving their lights around the area, but nothing appeared. Malcolm felt a chill that didn't seem to be coming from the night air.

Prisha spoke softly. "If there was something moving out there, we would hear it."

Malcolm shivered again. "I don't care. Let's get out of here. I don't want to be around bears."

"They won't harm you unless you're bothering them or if they have cubs nearby," Barry spoke with a voice that sounded as if he was trying to convince himself as well as the others. "And this is not the season for cubs. The bears shouldn't bother us."

"Tell that to Phillippe," Prisha said, softly.

Barry reached back and dropped his knapsack. "What am I thinking? We should be filming this." He kneeled down and began undoing the straps.

"I want to leave," Malcolm said.

"This won't take long," Barry said, pulling out his camera. "Besides, we'll turn on the camera lights and it won't be as spooky. Should scare away any animals, too."

Malcolm pulled his phone out of his pocket and clicked on the recording app. Prisha quickly assembled her camera and soon had the lights ready and indicated the same to everyone. Barry walked toward her and then handed his camera to Malcolm. "You guys just film me for a minute or so and I can describe what is going on. Malcolm, get a different angle. Then we'll just do some shots of the area we can edit in later."

Sighing, Malcolm took the camera and looked for an appropriate angle for filming.

Barry waited until Prisha was ready and then began speaking. "So our investigation led us here, to the camp where the kids said they saw the Gugwe. As you can see, it looks pretty peaceful. They have a nice little tree fort and a rope swing, and it appears they kept the place very clean. In fact, if you follow me…" He walked around the area, extending his arms. "…you can see that there doesn't seem to be any sign of a fight or a scuffle, or anything to show that there was even an encounter."

"Well, that's not fair," Prisha said. "It's been a week and a half and it's autumn and lots of leaves have fallen since then…"

"Don't interrupt, please," Barry said. "Now we have to edit all that out."

Prisha lowered the camera and stopped filming, concentrating her efforts on giving Barry a nasty look.

"Okay, fine," Barry said. "I'll mention that. Just start up again. But get a different angle so the edit won't look too bad."

Once he saw that Prisha was ready, he continued. "Admittedly, it's early fall and we're up north where the leaves fall much earlier than… hold on, that sounds bad. I shouldn't use 'fall' twice like that. Start again, and I'll say 'autumn' this time."

"Wait, what's that?" Malcolm held his light steady. In the distance, behind Barry, something glowed. Something red. Near the ground. Not moving. Not eyes.

Barry gave a deep sigh. "Well, let's go see. Prisha, keep filming." He stepped forward slowly, his light before him, as Prisha and Malcolm followed behind. Malcolm shivered again, but he wasn't sure if it was from the misty night breeze or from nerves.

"Let's see what Malcolm has found," Barry said to the camera. He reached the point Malcolm had and looked down. "Bikes," he announced, waving Prisha forward to get a better view.

Three bikes lay on the ground in perfect precision, as if they had originally been standing together but had fallen during the week and were now lying in wait for their owners to come back. Leaves, twigs, and other recently fallen items covered them. The red reflectors under the seats beamed back happily in the light.

"The kids saw the thing and ran, leaving the bikes," Prisha said, while filming the scene. "What we really need to do is figure out which way they would have run."

Malcolm ran his hand through his hair. "Well, if it was me, I would have gone to the path."

Prisha pouted. "What if, you know, the thing was in their way?"

"We can speculate all we want," Barry said. "But we won't know unless we look for signs to show where they ran. What direction. I mean, maybe there'll be broken branches and other indications."

"Brilliant, Sherlock," Prisha said, but she followed alongside, moving slowly to examine the ground, looking for clues. She continued filming.

Malcolm didn't feel as comfortable. He joined in the search but didn't stray too far from the others. "I feel like we're being watched," he said.

Barry scoffed. "That's just your paranoia. I'm sorry I said anything about seeing eyes. I mean, I never heard any noises of movement. I probably just imagined it."

"A dark, cloudy, autumn night with no moonlight doesn't help," Prisha added, staring at the ground. "It would be, you know, creepy even if we weren't in the area where a possible monster was seen, but a boy disappeared, and Barry thought he saw *eyes*."

"Yes, well, repeating all that doesn't help, either." Malcolm pulled his hood up to keep himself from shivering. Pushing through the brush, he swung his flashlight beam left and right, looking for anything unusual. Walking slowly, his mind racing with crazy horror-movie thoughts, he couldn't help but be worried. In the movies, this was when the monster would do a jump scare and the stupid kids would scream and then one would die, with the lesson being "Don't be so stupid as to search the woods that a big, scary monster is known to inhabit." This was his fault, he knew — too many sleepless nights watching those silly films.

Was it his imagination, or did there seem to be signs of passage before him? Broken branches at eye level, plants crushed beneath feet below, and the sort of things a city boy would imagine showed indications of someone running through the woods? Malcolm grunted. What did he know? Could have been a deer running through here. He walked slower though, just in case…

Before him was some sort of spiky plant that looked very dangerous and uncomfortable to touch, but there was a clear breaking, like someone or something burst through it not too long ago. He slowly crept forward and pushed them aside, like parting a curtain. A sharp decline into a dry ditch lay behind the brush. Malcolm pointed his light down into the darkness. His eyes widened and heart began pounding in his chest.

"Barry! Prisha!" he yelled. "Come here!"

Behind him, he could hear the two rapidly approaching, but he could not stop staring ahead.

"What is it?" Barry said, coming up from behind.

Malcolm swallowed. "I… I think I found Phillipe."

Chapter Nine

Prisha aimed her camera with its blaring light down the chasm as Barry leaned over her shoulder to look. There, at the bottom, was the body of a teenage boy. Leaves and twigs covered parts, and the rotting smell indicated that it had been there a while. Malcolm turned away, bile rising in his throat. He did not need to see more. He liked a good scary movie, but not the gory ones. And even those were just faked, and everyone knew it.

"We appeared to have found Phillippe," Barry said to the camera. "From what I can see from here, he fell and hit his head on some rocks—but then again, I think I see, uh, wounds that would not have come from a fall. Like an animal…"

"But we can't tell if that is recent, you know, from after or before the fall," Prisha said, moving the camera from the unpleasant scene to point instead at Barry.

Barry swallowed. Malcolm had to admit he had never seen Barry look so disturbed, but Barry also seemed determined to continue with the recording. "Although none of us are experts in this, it certainly appears that Philippe was killed by a fall as he was running away, and not from a Gugwe or other creature," he said. "This tends to support our theory that the kids saw a bear and ran away."

"No, it doesn't," Prisha said. "They could have seen a Gugwe and ran…"

Barry put on the sarcastic face that Malcolm knew so well. "We have two options. Either it was a natural animal that many have seen in this area often or it's a fantastic creature from mythology that we have absolutely no concrete evidence actually exists. I'm going with the option that is ninety-nine percent more likely."

"Enough," Malcolm said. "We have to call the police." He hit his phone app and then noticed that there was no signal.

"We shouldn't get closer or touch him," Prisha said. "They might think we did this."

"Don't be ridiculous," Barry said, but Malcolm could tell he was feigning his normal confidence. "They know we came here after he disappeared. But if we talk to the police, they'll know we disobeyed them. This time, we really are guilty of trespassing."

Malcolm placed his phone back in his pocket. "I think finding the body they've been looking for all this time is more important."

"No, we don't have to tell anyone," Prisha said. "Let's just sneak back to the motel. Remember, Nathan's mom was going to tell the police where this campsite is, and then they'll find it. It will be easier in the day, too, you know."

Barry nodded. "Suppose so."

Prisha turned off her camera. "I feel like we should say something over his body."

Barry began walking away, his flashlight scanning the ground before him. "Why? We're all atheists. Can't be a real skeptic otherwise. No such thing as a religious skeptic."

Prisha looked at Malcolm, shrugged, and then followed Barry back toward the campsite.

One last look around the camp found nothing else of interest, so the unspoken agreement was to return. Malcolm wasn't complaining. He was exhausted and needed sleep, although he wasn't sure if he would be able to. The image of Philippe's body kept flashing across his mind.

The walk back to the van seemed to take twice as long as the walk to the camp, but that may have been because no one was talking. Malcolm imagined that the other two were also disturbed by their discovery. It was the first time Malcolm had ever seen a dead body, and he just hoped it would be the last.

He was lost in his thoughts when he heard Barry say, "Uh oh."

Bright lights beamed through the trees below. Before anyone could react, one shone right into their eyes. Malcolm held his hand before his face.

"Somehow, I knew I'd find you here," Captain Picard said. He stood with his arms crossed, a cruel smile on his face. Two other officers stood nearby, yawning. Down at the dirt road, two police cars blocked Barry's van from leaving. The cars were running, and their headlights lit the forest, both reducing the spookiness of the situation and increasing it by their mere presence.

"Oh, good!" Prisha said, walking forward. "We were just going to get you. We tried calling, but—"

Picard waved her away. "This time, I think the judge will agree that you are trespassing."

"It's a public park!" Prisha replied. "People camp here—"

Barry pushed past her and interrupted. "This is more important, captain. We found Phillippe."

Picard stepped back; brow furrowed. After a second, he said, "What's this trick?"

"No trick," Malcolm said, pulling out his phone. "Look." He quickly found the video footage and held it up for Picard to see. "We're not sure if he fell running away or was attacked before or after or maybe animals got to his body…"

Picard's eyes widened at the image of Phillipe's body at the bottom of the crevice. "Did you touch him? Where is he? Take me to him!"

"No, captain, we didn't touch." Malcolm put the phone away.

Barry pointed. "It's up a bit and then you have to walk."

Picard glanced at the dirt road, winding up the hill. He scratched his nose and then said, "Get in the car. We'll drive up to where you say we have to stop."

Malcolm walked to the police car. He could feel Barry resisting, but figured he had no choice. If Picard was lying to get them into the car so he could arrest them, it was going to happen no matter what Malcolm wanted. And maybe Picard actually believed them.

He pushed into the backseat of the police vehicle. It was comfortable enough, but the bars between the front seat and the back proved unnerving.

Prisha slid in next to him and placed her bag on her lap.

Barry got in, frowning mightily, and gave Prisha a look. She nodded down, and he noticed that she was indeed recording this entire encounter. Maybe the video of it wouldn't be that good, but at least they'd have audio. Malcolm smiled. He had to agree this would be good for the show.

Picard took the wheel and started slowly driving up the dirt road, passing the van. The other officers followed behind in their own vehicle.

"Tell me everything," Picard grumbled. "What were you three doing up there, and how did you find Phillippe?"

Barry coughed and looked at Malcolm, who nodded him on. "We had an, uh, informant who told us where to look."

Picard snorted. "Nathan."

Barry looked sheepish. "Well, yes…"

"I do my work," Picard said, as he steered around a fallen branch in the road. "I know you spoke to him, and I know he was up here with his friends. He never told us exactly where this happened, though. He just said he was so scared he couldn't remember exactly, so we didn't know where to look."

"He promised his mother he was going to tell you." Prisha said. "I think he was just afraid to let you know they set up a kind of campsite up here."

"Finding Phillippe a week ago would have been a lot more important!"

Prisha nodded. "He's just a kid. He didn't want to get into trouble. Don't get mad at him."

Picard grumbled under his breath. "This area is closed to the public. It's not an area they're allowed to hike in or camp in. Those kids weren't supposed to be here at all, and they knew it. We've had bear sightings in this area. And not too far from here, campers have reported bears taking their food and ripping their tents and blankets when they were out hiking. It's not a safe area for—"

"Boobies!" Malcolm pointed ahead.

Picard hit the brakes. "What the—"

"Boobies rock!" Malcolm said. "I mean, I know they do, but there, look. See those boulders that look like boobies? That's where we stop."

Picard stopped the car but didn't turn it off. "They don't look anything like boobies."

"Yes, they do," Malcolm said. "I mean, you have to see them from the right angle."

"And from the point of view of teenage boys," Barry added.

Prisha sighed. "Can we just get out and go and stop being so obsessed with boobies?"

Malcolm blushed, embarrassed, but pleased that no one would notice his discomfort in the darkness. When Picard pulled off his seatbelt and turned the car off, Malcolm opened the door and got out, making sure his phone was handy for recording.

Is it illegal to record someone when they're not aware they're being recorded? Malcolm suddenly felt a pinch of guilt. He wasn't sure of the answer, especially in Canada, but after a minute, decided that by the time they posted their story, they'd be back in the U.S. and there wasn't much of a chance of them being extradited over such a minor crime. If it was a crime.

Barry didn't wait for anyone. "This way," he said, his flashlight pointing to the hidden path behind the rocks. Picard strapped a light onto his belt and motioned for his fellow officers to follow behind Malcolm and Prisha, apparently afraid that this could be some sort of trick.

Malcolm looked at Prisha, who nodded that she was still recording. She held the camera at her side so it would not be obvious she was recording, but clearly the mic was picking up everything. Malcolm turned the flash on from his phone and pointed it ahead, hoping the officers would think he was merely lighting the way instead of recording everything.

Picard kept his eye on Barry in the lead. "I'm still angry with you for lying to me about leaving, but if you found Phillipe, that is, indeed, more important. His family needs closure."

Barry's shoulders rose and fell, but he didn't turn around. "I apologize, captain. I didn't lie. I... may have been misleading about our intentions, but I never meant to cause problems. And I'm pleased to hear that you realize how important finding Phillipe is."

"We really did try to call you as soon as we found him," Prisha said, "but, you know, there's no signal here." She frowned, probably realizing she was still saying "you know" too much.

Picard nodded but remained silent.

"Up here is the camp," Barry said, leading the way. "It's where the kids hung out. They didn't tell you about it because they —"

"I get it," Picard said. He seemed subdued, as if considering what he was going to say to Phillippe's parents. At that moment, Malcolm felt sorry for the man, and was glad that he wouldn't have to be the person delivering the news.

Upon reaching the clearing, Picard picked his light from his belt and shone it around, stopping at the tree fort and other additions the kids had made to the land. "So where did you find... Phillippe?"

"This way, sir," Barry said. The events of the night had certainly affected him as well. Malcolm knew Barry loved tweaking those in power and otherwise being what he thought was the epitome of the classic skeptic, but at this moment, the discovery of a dead body overshadowed everything.

Barry led them toward the cliff, pushing bushes and branches out of the way. Picard kept right up with him.

"Down there," Barry said, pointing to the crevice, unwilling to view that awful scene again. "That's where we saw him."

Picard walked past him and bent down, shining his light down the hill. He swung the light left and right, observing the area, his breathing slow. He then turned back, stared at Barry, and said, "What exactly are you trying to accomplish here?"

Although Malcolm could not see Barry's face, his body moved indicating stress. "I don't understand."

Picard pointed down into the chasm.

Malcolm and Prisha rushed up to join Barry as the three of them shone their lights down the hill.

The body was gone.

CHAPTER TEN

"It was there!" Barry said, pointing his flashlight down the chasm. "You saw the video. It was there!"

Picard snorted. "You could have faked that."

"With the massive CGI equipment I keep hidden in my pockets?" Prisha sneered. "Come on, be reasonable…"

"It could have been a dummy," Picard replied.

"You're the dummy," Barry said, pointing a finger at the officer. "Why would we fake that and then tell you about it and bring you right here to show you a dummy that would never fool you? Come on, be reasonable—there was a body here, and now it's gone. Someone took it."

"Or some*thing*," Malcolm said. He found himself shivering again.

Picard glared at Barry, but Malcolm could see that his emotions were mixed. Barry made sense. There would be no reason they would have lied about it.

Malcolm watched as Picard turned to his deputies, both of whom were clearly trying to show bravery. The three spoke quickly in French, but Malcolm clearly made out the word "Gugwe."

"Come on," Barry said. "Prisha, film this. We need to check it out."

Prisha pulled up her camera, flicked on the light, and started filming Barry as he grabbed at branches and started down the steep incline.

"I'm not going down there," Malcolm said. "Do you want what happened to Phillipe happen to you?"

"It's okay," Barry said. "I'm sure it was just a bear or something. Maybe a wolf dragged the body off. Besides, we have officers here with guns, which Phillipe didn't have."

"Why now, after we found the body?" Malcolm asked. "Why not a week ago? And what about the eyes you saw?"

Picard turned to Malcolm. "Eyes?"

"Barry thought he saw eyes in the darkness watching us," Malcolm said. "Human-height. Not low to the ground."

The officers with Picard shuffled nervously and one reached for her pistol, as if to confirm to herself that it was still there. Picard frowned, stepped forward, and peered over the edge. He turned off his light and placed it in its compartment on his belt to free his hands. Then, without a word, he began following Barry's path. The two deputies glanced at each other and then trudged along behind.

"I'll stay up here, thank you," said Prisha.

"And I'll, uh, protect Prisha," Malcolm said, looking around to make sure nothing was coming from behind. It seemed to him that things had changed very quickly. What was once a calm, peaceful forest on a brisk autumn night had morphed into a spooky, chilling landscape with ominous clouds, bare trees waving their tendril-like branches at him, and a sharp breeze causing fallen leaves to rustle and grab at his legs.

"Do you notice that?" he asked Prisha.

"Shh," she said. "I'm recording."

"But that's just it," he replied. "It's really quiet all of a sudden. Like, no sounds of crickets or owls or anything. Just the rushing water from the falls."

She looked at him and winked, and then mouthed, "Great! Build up the tension."

Malcolm stared at her to let her know that was not his intention, but she had turned back to watch what Barry and the officers were doing. His shoulder tensing, Malcolm turned his attention below where that Barry and the officers were pointing their lights at the ground and otherwise examining the scene.

"Prisha, you need to get down here and film this," Barry said.

"What? Film?" Picard looked up. "You're filming this?"

Although it was dark, Malcolm couldn't see Barry's expression, but his body language made it clear he wasn't happy with his surprise. "Uh, yes, captain. For our show. You don't mind, do you? I think… people will be happy to see the police take charge here and solve this, don't you?"

Picard let out a laugh. "Trying to butter me up, are you? Fine, you can record—it will help in the long run when we have to explain to everyone what happened. But if I say stop, you stop, understood?"

Malcolm let out the breath he didn't realize he was holding, and then touched Prisha on the shoulder. She glanced up at him and he indicated that they should follow the others. She nodded, and then the two of them slowly climbed down the hill, holding onto each other for safety. As they descended, the sounds of the falls grew louder and filled their ears, echoing off the cliffside. Malcolm even felt as if spray was hitting his face, although he could not see any water.

Once at the bottom, Prisha pulled out the camera, turned on the light, and resumed filming. Picard was on his knees next to Barry while the two other officers stood by, eyes on the surroundings.

"Look here," Picard said to the camera, as if he was now the host of the show. "Here's signs of where the body was, as well as what looks like dried blood on this rock. We'll send our team over to check it more thoroughly in the morning. See these marks? Someone dragged the body off in that direction." He stood and started walking that way, and then paused. Pulling out his flashlight, he aimed it at the ground and then spun it around the area. "But now there's nothing. No signs of anything."

"What does that mean?" Prisha asked.

Picard looked at the camera and spoke as if he was one of the talking heads on some news show. "It means whoever took the body picked it up and walked away with it, instead of dragging it."

"So not a wolf," Malcolm said.

"And not a bear," Picard said.

Barry jumped in front of Picard, placing himself in clear view of the camera. "So you're telling me some human did this? One of the kids perhaps? Someone who may have been trying to play a trick on us? Maybe the body was indeed a dummy all along and we couldn't tell from our distance at night—"

"I am not speculating at all," Picard said, cutting Barry off. "I'm just saying what the evidence before me indicates right now, which could change when we have real experts come in to process the scene. Isn't that what you skeptics do? Hold off on coming to conclusions without evidence?"

"Of course," Barry said, instantly. "Which is why no one should be coming to any conclusion yet, and especially one that involves amazing monsters when a simpler explanation is possible."

Picard fixed his eye on Barry for a few seconds, gave a snort, and then said, "It's not like we can track anything right now. We'll have to wait until daylight. I'll call dispatch to send out the crime scene investigators. You three, in the meantime, are to leave. I'll forget this trespass happened, especially if we find Phillippe, but I don't want to see you around. Understand? Go back home. You've got your story."

"But—" Prisha said.

"No, listen. I could have you all arrested right now. Judge Bellanger will not be happy to see you again and will probably place a high bail on you. Don't be a dummy, as your friend here called me. Leave now. We'll take care of this from here."

Prisha grumbled but kept filming. Malcolm was just happy for the officer's threat—he was more than anxious to get back to the motel and then head back home. They had enough to make a show with now.

"Wait, what's that?" Barry said, as he rushed into the woods.

"Dummy," Picard said, watching Barry run off.

"Look, it's a piece of clothing stuck on a branch," Barry said from a distance. "That means they went this way!" He shone his light before him and ran around an outcropping.

"Barry, get back here!" Malcolm found himself yelling. "Don't you ever watch monster movies? You never split up the group!"

Picard had already started following Barry's path, cursing in French. Prisha followed, filming constantly, and Malcolm had to hurry to keep up. The two officers stayed behind Malcolm, flashlights scanning the trees. He could tell they were following by the sounds of their feet against the leaves.

Malcolm heard Picard's voice from around the outcropping. "Well, now what?"

"Oh, my," Prisha said.

Malcolm turned to find a beautiful waterfall spraying mist into his face. Prisha and Picard were shining their lights left and right.

And Barry was nowhere to be found.

Chapter Eleven

Malcolm and Prisha screamed Barry's name but there was no response.

"The noise of the waterfall is too great for him to hear you, I guess." Picard scratched his nose as he and the other officers searched the ground for any clues to Barry's location. They especially targeted the stream, where water rushed downhill after escaping the falls.

"In the video games, there's always a secret passage behind the waterfall," Malcolm said. Everyone ignored him.

Prisha faced the camera toward Picard. "What are you going to do, captain?"

Picard looked as if he was about to say something insulting back to her, but then paused and looked thoughtful. Malcolm imagined him considering the possibility of this being broadcast, allowing him to be the hero. In the darkness of the night, he could almost see a change in the officer's demeanor, in the way he stood taller and appeared more confident.

"We don't need to find another dead body," he slowly said to the camera. "I'll have my deputies call for backup, and while we wait for them to arrive, we'll continue the search. He couldn't have gone far. You two need to get back down to your van and leave this to the professionals."

Prisha's voice cracked a bit, but she attempted to remain professional. "What do you think happened?"

"My worry is that, like Phillippe, he fell and hurt himself and that's why he's not responding." He raised an eyebrow. "So let's start our search downstream in case he fell and was carried away."

Malcolm shook his head. "No, look behind the waterfall." Once more, they ignored him as the deputies spoke rapidly in French.

Picard frowned and then spoke to the camera once again. "My deputies have tried to contact HQ but there is a lot of static—not sure if they heard us. These damn things don't work half the time, and of course, the budget doesn't allow…" He paused, apparently realizing he shouldn't be badmouthing whoever was in charge of the budget, and then continued. "We're wasting time. If he's in trouble, we need to find him. Everybody follow me. This way, following the water, back toward the van." He turned, pointed his flashlight at the running water, and began traveling downstream, staying on the banks except when the brush proved too thick. His deputies followed.

"I'm going to check the waterfall," Malcolm said.

Prisha nodded; eyes wide. "If you, you know, insist. You'll get soaked. I'm not leaving you alone, though. If you hit a wall, come right back. If you get through, I'll follow, but, you know, turning off the camera."

Malcolm placed his phone deep into his pocket, took a deep breath, and hoped for the best. Holding his hands before him, he plunged into the water and reached through the waterfall, expecting to find a wall of dirt or stone. He reached a little farther, stepped forward then reached even farther, only to realized he was indeed on the other side of the falls. "Well, whaddya know," he mumbled. "Just like in a game."

"Malcolm? Where are you?"

He called out to be heard over the falls. "Here, but wait a minute." He pulled out his phone, started to wipe it on his sleeve, and realized there was nothing dry about him. Fortunately, the phone still worked, and he switched on the flashlight app. He shone it before the blurry scene, then kneeled down and placed it on the ground face up so the light shone toward the ceiling. He felt around in his backpack and then pulled out a cloth that he used to wipe his glasses the best he could. Placing them back on, he stared through them at the scene.

Stalactites hung from the ceiling of a small cave, which appeared to have been carved out of the rocks by millions of years of water. The smoothness of the walls and floors reminded him of cavern tours, where it almost felt unnatural, as if someone had taken the time to polish the walls and floors. However, unlike the tourist caves Malcolm liked to visit, these were dirty and covered in cobwebs. Still, his childhood interest in caves held his attention as he admired the view.

"Come in, but be careful," he said. "It's slippery."

Uneven areas of the floor made walking difficult, but he headed back toward the falls and held his hand out. As Prisha stepped through, soaked like him, he grabbed her arm and helped her gain her footing.

She wiped her eyes, pulled wet hair off her face, and stared at the scene for a few seconds before reaching into her backpack. "Camera seems okay," she reported. "But I'm worried it may have been hurt from the water." She pulled out her flashlight, turned it on, and then surveyed the cave. "Ooh, ick, spiders."

"We won't film unless we find something," Malcolm said. He shone his light back and forth. Where he may have been shivering before from fear, he now found himself shivering from cold, as the freezing water dripped off him. He considered turning back, but knew he had to find Barry.

Prisha called out their friend's name, which echoed eerily in the caves.

"Hear that?" Malcolm said. "Sounds like there are passages beyond this."

Prisha sniffed and wiped her nose. "If you say so."

"No, I used to go spelunking. I can tell," he said, without mentioning that his cave exploration consisted of guided tours through safe caverns frequented by tourists. He aimed his light around the area. An unusual shadow grabbed his attention. "I think there's an opening over there."

Stepping carefully to avoid slipping, Malcolm gently tiptoed to the spot. "Yes… there is an opening here, but you have to duck to get through it."

Prisha inched up next to him. "I'm not so sure about this. What if there really is a Gugwe and it grabbed Barry and took him here? Shouldn't we get the police and let them do this?"

Malcolm paused. He had been so excited about discovering the cave he had not considered the danger. "Um, good point." He pointed his light into the crevice. "On the other hand, if Barry fell and is hurt, and we don't do what we can to find him in time, well, I'm not sure I could live with myself for not at least trying."

"He'd never let you hear the end of it," Prisha admitted.

They looked into each other's eyes for a second and then, with silent agreement, bent down and slowly walked through the crevice. The echoes from their footsteps changed dramatically, and as they rose to their full height, they could tell that this new area was larger and taller.

The ground remained uneven, but it was also dryer and easier to gain their footing. A sweep of the light indicated a number of other passages had been carved from the stone from years of water traveling through. Most of them were way too small for anyone—or any *thing*—to traverse.

Malcolm held his finger before his mouth, and Prisha nodded her agreement. If there was the slightest possibility that a bear or even a Gugwe was involved, it was probably better not to call attention to themselves. That thought made Malcolm's mouth dry, and he tried to swallow a few times with little success.

A poke to his back made him jump, but it was just Prisha grabbing his attention. She pointed her flashlight to the ground and raised an eyebrow. Malcolm looked.

It was Barry's cell phone. Its light had gone out, but there was no mistaking it.

Malcolm indicated to Prisha that she should keep an eye on the possible openings to other cavernous areas, and then he slowly walked toward the phone and picked it up. The screen had been cracked, and Malcolm's attempts to turn it on proved futile. He placed it in a pocket and looked to Prisha, whose expression projected a forced bravery covering absolute fear.

"If he had just dropped it, he would have picked it up," Malcolm whispered. "Something happened."

Prisha nodded her agreement, eyes wide.

Malcolm gathered up his courage, which was not easy. He'd never seen himself as the heroic type—even in his computer games, he liked to play the scholarly wizard instead of the manly fighter running into battle. He hadn't even liked gym class, where the other kids made fun of his geeky awkwardness. Taking a deep breath, he forced himself to step forward to check out the possible paths Barry may have taken.

The first one he came to seemed promising. He could walk through the passageway without having to stoop down or turn sideways. Then he paused. "Uh oh."

Prisha had remained close behind. "What is it?"

"Look at this." Malcolm pointed his light at the opening. "This isn't natural. Someone—or some thing—has carved into the stone to make it easier to walk through."

Prisha stepped back a bit. "I think we should leave and let the experts handle this."

"But what if Barry is in trouble?"

"He'll understand. Look, this isn't a bear. Bears don't carve cave walls. This shows some intelligence. And that makes me even more scared." She took another step backward.

Malcolm once more had trouble swallowing. "Okay, maybe you're right. We're not equipped for dealing with this."

He turned around and motioned for Prisha to lead the way back out. They pointed their lights ahead of them and took a few steps. Malcolm kept his eyes low, not wanting to trip over loose rocks or wet spots. He grunted when he bumped into Prisha, who had stopped in her path. He looked up.

Two red eyes glowed in the passageway before them, about seven or eight feet off the ground.

And then the eyes started moving toward them.

Chapter Twelve

Their screams echoed through the cavern. Malcolm turned around and ran. The back of mind knew this was only leading deeper into the cave but trying to get out meant passing the creature. Was it a bear? Was it the Gugwe? He wasn't about to stick around to find out.

His feet slipped and knocked against walls and stalagmites. His pants ripped as they caught and dislodged rocks. The light from the phone in his hand bounced off the walls in all directions, as if he was running a marathon through a discotheque. At one point, he banged his head and smashed his nose against the wall—and then, suddenly, he was falling, phone slipping from his fingers. He slid down an embankment, only to land face first in an underground pool.

Turning over, he listened for any sounds of pursuit. Realizing he was holding his breath, he let it out. The pool was less than a foot deep, and tremendously cold. His phone's light had gone out, and he could see nothing in the pitch dark. He felt around in the water, but couldn't locate it, and gave up before his hands froze off.

Prisha was nowhere to be found.

He blinked, reached up to his face, and realized his glasses were gone as well. He had a spare set, but they were back at the motel.

Standing slowly, he stretched his arms out. From the sound of the water around his feet and its echoing off the walls, he could tell that he was in a large cave. He walked in the direction he imagined he had come from, but in the darkness and confusion, could not be sure. However, a few steps brought him out of the pool of water.

Sliding one foot before the other was the safest way to move forward without tripping over something. After a few feet, he could tell that the passageway sloped upward, and he hoped that was the way he had found himself here.

Too bad I'm not a believer, or I'd be praying right now, he thought. *I wish we atheists had something stupidly magical to calm us when there was trouble.*

He stopped to take off his backpack and empty it of as much water as he could. Fortunately, the thing was made to be waterproof from rain, but even the best waterproof backpack couldn't handle being dunked into a pool. As he knelt down and examined its contents by feel alone, he discovered his prized donuts were still mostly dry, although somewhat crushed. *Well, at least that's a good thing*, he thought ironically. *I won't starve, although I may get sugar poisoning.*

He stayed there, kneeling, with his hands grasping the backpack like a life preserver, and pondered his situation, with thoughts and questions racing through his mind. What should he do? Should he wait for someone to find him? Maybe Picard would come back up and realize where they had gone. But what if Prisha was hurt or worse, captured by whatever that thing was? Was it a Gugwe or just a bear? Or someone just trying to scare them? Did he just imagine it? No, Prisha saw it. If he went back, the thing might get him, too, but if he stayed in one place, it might hunt him down. On the other hand, if he moved, it would make noise that could grab its attention. And, wait a minute, why would there be just one? If it was indeed the *Arctodus simus*, then that meant there had to be more than one, because it had to reproduce to still be here thousands of years later.

He let out a great sigh. And then blinked as a sound caught his ear.

Was that water dripping steadily, or was that something else?

He strained to listen. It sounded like… drums. Like something was playing a drum. Way off, in the distance, directionless and muffled. Unlike the steady dripping of water, this had patterns and a rhythm that could never be natural.

Something was drumming. In the cave.

His mind reeled, imagining so many old black-and-white movies where the natives drummed for King Kong, and then Tarzan saved the day or something, he wasn't sure. But what did that mean? Were there primitive humans here in the cave, not too far from a Canadian suburb?

Or was the Gugwe… *intelligent*?

And had he just gone from complete skepticism about its existence to considering the possibility more than just a silly dream? Could the thing actually exist?

Or… what if that was Barry trying to send a message that he thought someone might hear? Yes. Yes, that was much more likely, and, as all skeptics know, you assume the more likely possibility unless evidence convinces you otherwise.

But there were those eyes glowing in the flashlight's beam…

Not knowing what else to do, and afraid of just staying put and waiting for something to come and get him, Malcolm began moving slowly up the slope. Grabbing at the walls allowed him to maintain his balance, but in the darkness, he was hesitant to move too quickly. And even if he had a light, without his glasses, almost everything more than a few feet ahead of him would be blurry and indistinguishable. His heart skipped a beat a few times when he lost his footing, but he eventually found himself at the top of the slope, where the ground was dryer and movement was easier.

Although he wasn't sure which direction the sound came from, he kept his hand on the left wall and moved forward, which reminded him of the computer games with labyrinths that were impossible mazes where all you could do was keep to one direction until you either wound up where you started or found a new room—although hopefully, there wouldn't be a minotaur waiting for him.

Just a Gugwe.

Or a bunch of them.

Swallowing again, and not knowing what else to do, he continued on.

It was difficult to estimate the time. Had he been here only minutes or an hour? Malcolm never wore a watch and relied on his phone to tell him the time. And even if he had a watch, he thought, how would he be able to read it in the darkness, without his glasses?

He pushed on, step by step.

A few times, his hands ran into spiderwebs, once causing him to fall back, losing his balance. He recovered, cursing himself, but also thankful that he hadn't walked straight into one. *At least I haven't had to deal with bats*, he thought. *With my luck, I'll discover that vampires are real, too.*

Were the drums getting louder? He strained to listen, and wondered where Prisha might be. Did she hear the drums too? Was she heading in that direction? Had she run back out to get help? Was she even alive? What if she fell and hurt herself?

He tried to get those terrible images out of his mind. He had to keep moving. Maybe he'd come across her and could help, but staying put certainly would solve nothing.

He continued on, step by step, staying to the left but hearing the drums echoing off the walls, as if he was nearing their source.

He blinked. Was there light ahead? He paused, strained, and realized that there was indeed flickering light, off in the distance, being reflected on the water dripping down the walls.

Summoning up the best of his courage, he continued on, the drums reverberating off the slimy walls, sounding like something from a bad Phil Spector mix in the '60s.

He ducked down. There. Ahead. An opening. Large enough for someone or something to walk through without a problem. The light and the drums came from there.

Despite the fact that he was wet and shivering, his face felt hot. He stayed low, moving slowly.

And peeked through the opening.

It was not at all what he expected.

Chapter Thirteen

It took Malcolm a bit to focus and consider what he was seeing. Without his glasses, everything was blurry, but what really took the time was making his mind accept what appeared before him.

A large cave, well-lit by a roaring fire in the center. Smoke rising through vents in the ceiling. Bedrolls, cans of food, tarps, and other camping gear decorated the floors and walls, making the place look almost comfortable.

And sitting around the fire were… well… half a dozen Gugwe.

There was just no other explanation. It had to be them.

Some were larger, some small, and two appeared to be children. An older-looking Gugwe was tapping on one of those cheap tom-tom kits they sell in department stores.

Malcolm's heart felt like it would beat through his chest. The Gugwe *lived* here. They existed. And they apparently survived by stealing camping supplies from tourists, or maybe just from finding things left behind.

Straining to see more, Malcolm leaned forward.

And then the drums stopped.

He held his breath as the Gugwe slowly turned toward him.

Their faces were dog-like, but distinguishable from one another. Clean fur covered their bodies. Their eyes held no anger, but a sense of curiosity. They watched him, waiting. For something. Taking no action.

Malcolm stood. There was no need to hide now.

And that's when he heard the voice.

"Malcolm? You're okay?"

Turning slowly, Malcolm located Barry through blurry vision. Barry then stood, appearing disheveled but unharmed.

"I know, right?" Barry said. "They kind of chased me here and sort of made it clear they wanted me to stay and then… showed me this." He pointed to a lump of blankets on the ground.

"What is it?"

"It's… Phillipe," Barry said. "I think they were doing some sort of ritual over his dead body. They wrapped him up and started playing the drums and I didn't want to interrupt them."

Malcolm swallowed. "Well, that's not creepy at all."

"Sarcasm noted." Barry shifted his feet uncomfortably. "Don't suppose you have your phone with you…"

"No, lost somewhere." Malcolm tried to look brave, but it was difficult. Were the Gugwe friendly, or were they just biding their time, watching, waiting for something? "What do they want?" he finally asked.

Barry seemed to slump a bit, but Malcolm could not discern his expression. After a few seconds, Barry said, "I guess they want us to take him. They've wrapped him up the best they could."

Malcolm didn't know how to respond to that. "Do they… talk? Do they understand you?"

Barry nodded his head. "No. They're like… real intelligent apes. I'll bet if you got one of those devices they use to talk to the apes like that one had, Koko or whatever his name was…"

The largest of the Gugwe suddenly stood, which caused Barry to back up and remain silent. Malcolm also took a step back, until he felt his shoulders hit the uneven walls of the cavern.

For a few seconds, no one moved, and then the Gugwe began walking toward Malcolm.

For reasons he could not later explain, Malcolm pulled off his backpack, struggled a bit, and pulled out a soggy donut. He held it out to the Gugwe.

It stopped, stared at the presentation of the baked good, and then spent a long time gazing into Malcolm's eyes. Malcolm froze, afraid to move, regretting that he had even done such a thing. What if giving someone a donut was seen as an insult in whatever consisted of Gugwe society? What if it took the donut and hated it? What if the Gugwe thought it was poisoned?

The Gugwe reached out. Its arms were so long, they could reach Malcolm's outstretched hand, bypass it, and grab him by the neck.

Instead, the Gugwe slowly took the donut from Malcolm's hand, slowly brought it to its nose and sniffed, and then took a bite.

Its expression did not change, but it walked forward as if it was heading to the massive room's opening. Malcolm moved to the side to allow it to pass. The smell of the creature was musty and pungent, like a wet dog. It continued to take small bites from the donut as it passed by. Malcolm tried not to show any emotion, but he felt as if he was about to fall apart inside.

It was then he heard the yelling. Muffled, and echoed, in the distance.

Prisha was coming, calling their names.

The Gugwe stood at the entrance to the area, staring, waiting for the newcomers. It did not have a weapon, but Malcolm figured if it got into a fight, it wouldn't need one.

Malcolm glanced at Barry and then stepped forward, facing the Gugwe, who towered over him by at least a foot. "I know you can't understand me," he said, "but hopefully the tone of my voice will calm you and let you know that my friend is coming, and she'll not hurt anyone." He held his hands in what he thought might be a peaceful manner. "Allow me to go and greet her before she gets here." Backing up slowly, he bumped against the opening and then turned and walked away, hoping against odds that the Gugwe wouldn't decide to attack him from behind.

It was a surreal experience, as if he was merely dreaming it. This was real? Were they actually *Arctodus simus*? This would be the archeological finding of the century...

Lights danced against the wet walls and Malcolm was able to better choose his footing. He walked slowly, not just to avoid uneven ground, but also because everything was still fuzzy, adding to the dream-like nature of it all.

"Prisha!" he called, in as low a voice as possible, in the hopes the echoes would carry it through the cavernous passageways.

As he continued on, hand to the wall for steady support, he turned to find not just Prisha, but also Picard and his two assistants. Before they could speak, he held up a hand.

"Don't go any farther until I explain," he said.

Prisha's eyes were wide. "Are you okay? Are you hurt? Where are your glasses?"

"Yes, no, I don't know, but that's not important now. Captain, this is serious."

Picard shone his light past Malcolm, and twisted his head to see what was beyond, but remained silent, waiting to hear what Malcolm wanted.

So Malcolm told them.

And, to Malcolm's surprise, Captain Picard nodded. He then moved ahead, toward the crevice leading to the large area, passing Malcolm and Prisha. The two deputies shone their lights ahead, one sweeping it along the floor to indicate that the two skeptics should follow.

Malcolm found himself holding his breath as they re-entered the brightly lit area. The Gugwe at the entrance moved aside for them but watched Malcolm closely, which made his hair stand on end. He watched as the other Gugwe rose and looked at Picard, clearly recognizing him.

Picard took a few seconds to take in the scene and then his eyes lit upon the swaddled form before the fire. He caught the eyes of his deputies and nodded his head in that direction, and the two moved forward, attached their lights to their belts, and slowly lifted Phillippe's body. They turned and carried it out, somber-faced, but clearly uncomfortable with both the task and the smell.

Picard gave a nod to the large Gugwe who remained by the entrance and then quietly said, "Let's go." He turned to follow his deputies and didn't look back. Malcolm exchanged quick glances with Prisha and Barry and then followed, not wanting to remain behind without a light. He could hear his friends behind.

"Prisha!" Barry whispered. "You should be filming this!"

Prisha didn't respond, but Malcolm imagined the look she gave Barry. Everyone remained quiet as they backed through the maze-like caverns and emerged into the moonless night.

"We need to talk," Barry said to Picard.

"No," Picard said. "Not now. We need to take care of Phillipe and report to his family. We'll talk after, I promise." He spun around and pointed a finger at Barry. "And you will not post a damn thing about this, understand?"

"But..."

"You do, and we'll have you deported so fast and have your visa taken and make you look like the kind of person you are always insulting on your stupid show, get it?" Picard nodded for his deputies to continue toward the car. They grumbled something in French but continued on, their belt flashlights bouncing with each step. Picard then took his light and shone it right in Barry's face. Malcolm had to step to the side to see anything, but Barry remained stubbornly still.

"I am not threatening you," Picard said. "I'm merely warning you. These peaceful creatures have lived here longer than any of us, and there is a reason we keep this area free from tourists and campers and spread stories of bear attacks. We help the Gugwe and do our best to leave them alone, because if the world found out, they would never have peace."

Barry opened his mouth, but Picard leaned forward and spoke a bit more forcefully. "Yes, we encourage the fun Gugwe souvenirs and otherwise joke about it, but that money is used to keep them safe and fed in the winter."

Barry raised his arms imploringly. "Biologists would want to…"

"…study them and ruin their natural habitat," Picard finished. "Yes, we know that. The Canadian government knows that. But imagine that was you—you're just trying to raise your family and live peacefully. I mean, come on, these beings are friggin' vegetarians most of the time. They're not causing harm to anyone. They're as intelligent as, well, dogs at least. Leave them the hell alone, okay? We don't want them to end up like whales at Sea World or in a zoo or something."

"I agree," said Prisha.

Barry stared at her. "But the scientific community…"

"…can wait," Picard said. "Listen to your friend. I have a strong feeling that if you were to report what you've found, your friends here would disavow you and treat you like some sort of conspiracy-mad fool. Am I right?"

Barry had kept his eyes on Prisha, who refused to return his look. Raising an eyebrow, he transferred his gaze to Malcolm, waiting for a word that would contradict what Picard had said, and then gave a heavy sigh when none was forthcoming.

"I'm just happy that Phillipe was found and also very happy that none of you were hurt," Picard said. "In the dark, you could have fallen and killed yourself like Phillipe." He turned and began walking down the hill toward the vehicles. "You may not believe this, but I am thrilled you are unharmed. So come on. I have coffee and donuts back at the station."

Chapter Fourteen

"Hello, and welcome to another episode of 'Skeptic Soup.'" Barry smiled at the camera. "As you know, we took a few weeks off and had a wonderful vacation in Canada, so we apologize for not being here for you, but now, we have an exciting new investigation."

Malcolm watched as Barry walked backward into a field, keeping his face pointed toward Prisha's camera. "Crop circles! One has just appeared in a farmer's field here in upstate New York, and it's causing quite a stir. Is it from an alien intelligence trying to communicate? Or is it just merely a coincidence that the crops have all been harvested, and the field is empty for the winter and thus useless for anything except crop circles?" He winked. "I think you know what we'll find. So let's go see!"

He paused for a few seconds until Prisha indicated the camera was off.

"This is more like it," Malcolm said. "No big scary monsters, just charlatans and superstitions."

Barry groaned. "Yeah, don't keep rubbing it in. There's nothing I would have loved more than to be the journalist who discovered the Gugwe, but Picard was quite convincing. And those Gugwe looked like they wanted to be left alone."

Malcolm was actually proud of Barry. Prisha had suggested using the footage they had taken and then coming to the conclusion that the kids had mistaken a bear for a Gugwe, but Barry vetoed that. "That would be a lie, and we won't lie to our viewers. Instead, we'll just remain silent and no one has to know that we were doing an investigation."

Fortunately, as Prisha had never had the time to upload the teaser, none of Skeptic Soup's subscribers were even aware they had gone to Canada to investigate the Gugwe.

Barry kept walking until he reached the peak of the hill, which allowed him to look down on the crop circle, with its weird designs. He motioned for Prisha to continue filming. "There it is," he said, pointing for the camera. "We have two possibilities here. Either aliens in a UFO came all the way to earth and created this for unknown reasons, thus letting us know of their existence while still remaining hidden—" He paused for dramatic effect. "—or Farmer Alfalfa here discovered a new source of income to take from gullible morons paying to view it."

He walked toward the camera until his face filled the screen. "Join us as we have some fun with them on the next episode of 'Skeptic Soup'!"

About the Author

Michael A. Ventrella writes witty adventures like the Teddy Roosevelt steampunk novel *Big Stick* and the Terin Ostler fantasy series. He's edited over a dozen anthologies, including *Release the Virgins, Three Time Travelers Walk Into...*, and *The Baker Street Irregulars* series (with Jonathan Maberry). He has nonfiction books about The Beatles and The Monkees, and with Pulitzer Prize winner Darrin Bell, *How to Argue the Constitution with a Conservative*. He lives in the beautiful Pocono Mountains of Pennsylvania with his artist wife Heidi Hooper and four spoiled cats. In his spare time, he is an attorney. His web page is www.MichaelAVentrella.com.

artist's rendition of Gugwe

GUGWE

(Also known as Face Eater or Head Eater.)

ORIGINS: Said to inhabit dense and remote boreal forests in Canada, primarily Quebec and Labrador, though also reported in the Northwestern territories, where Gugwe activity is so pronounced there is a region called Headless Valley, or Valley of the Headless Men.

There is some theory that they are aquatic adaptation of Bigfoot due the number of sightings near bodies of water and a claimed fondness for fish.

There have been encounters reported in North America, primarily in Wisconsin, but also in the Appalachian Mountains and as far south as Texas.

DESCRIPTION: Accounts depict the Gugwe as a humanoid creature between six to eight feet tall, with fur ranging from white to grey to black, though a few accounts cite them as having red fur, in full or part.

Gugwe's most distinctive physical characteristics are a sagittal crest and protruding snout (dog-like or baboon-like) with large canines.

They have been reported to walk bipedally, but also on all fours, leaving a long track, narrow at the heel and dividing into two rounded toes at the front. Some report the toes to be webbed.

The other defining characteristics are a foul odor—some say fishlike—and its haunting, high-pitched cry.

Extremely aggressive and territorial in nature, Gugwe are reported to tear the heads off those trespassing and eating them. Indigenous tribes consider them very dangerous to humans, but mostly they are believed to hunt small creatures at night.

This cryptid has been associated with many others of a similar type, such as Yeti/Sasquatch/Bigfoot, Dogmen, Woodbooger, and Wendigo, primarily because of shared features: tall, furred, humanoid mix, bipedal nature. Its unique distinct differences, however, bring the Gugwe to be classified as its own creature, rather than a variant or subset of its more prominent cousins.

LIFE CYCLE: No definitive evidence has been found, and reports vary whether or not Gugwe are solitary creatures or live and travel in family groups, similar to the primates they resemble.

HISTORY: While accounts have been recorded in folklore for centuries, modern accounts do not begin until the 1900s.

The first documentation in writing appeared in Elliot Merrick's *True North*, published in 1933, recounting a young girl's harrowing encounter with a Gugwe in the Labrador region in 1913.

The creature was not captured on film until 1995, only discovered after the fact in the background of scenic shots taken in Seven Chutes, Quebec. Other accounts have been reported, with the most recent being in 2012, primarily from hikers.

While some theorize that the Gugwe is an escaped scientific experiment from either Canada or the US, there is no evidence to substantiate these claims.

About the Artist

Until his decades-long disappearance, JW Harp was known for his trippy underground comic strip *Captain Thetan*, about a seafarer who controls reality for himself and others. This otherworldly character appeared in a dozen issues of the classic rare underground zine *Sandanista Romp*. JW has reemerged thanks largely to eSpec Books' Systema Paradoxa series. In 2023, JW started Skilletfire Studios with comic-book author Scott Eckelaert. Under the Skilletfire Studios mantle, JW has produced the graphic novel *Boylon Heights*, and the *Gimme Five Comics* series. Since its launch, *Gimme Five Comics* has included work by Artyom Topilin, Elena Cerisciola, John L. French, Keith Lansdale, and Joe R. Lansdale with more to come.

JW grew up in the seedy parts of South Carolina, which is all of it. He feels part Canadian and part Costa Rican these days. He lives in North Carolina. Please get in touch with him at jwharp@skilletfire.com.

CAPTURE THE CRYPTIDS!

Cryptid Crate is a monthly subscription box filled with various cryptozoology and paranormal-themed items to wear, display, and collect. Expect a carefully curated box filled with creeptastic pieces from indie makers and artisans pertaining to bigfoot, sasquatch, UFOs, ghosts, and other cryptid and mysterious creatures (apparel, decor, media, etc).

Now Featuring Cryptid Crate Jr.!

http://CryptidCrate.com